MW00412231

1

Other books by Alex Ander:

Special Agent Cruz Crime Dramas:
Vengeance Is Mine (Book #1)
Defense of Innocents (Book #2)
Plea for Justice (Book #3)
Aaron Hardy Patriotic Thrillers:
The Unsanctioned Patriot (Book #1)
American Influence (Book #2)
Deadly Assignment (Book #3)
Patriot Assassin (Book #4)
The Nemesis Protocol (Book #5)
Necessary Means (Book #6)
Foreign Soil (Book #7)
Standalone:
The President's Man: Aaron Hardy Omnibus 1-3
The President's Man 2: Aaron Hardy Omnibus 4-6
Special Agent Cruz Crime Series
The First Agents

American Influence

Patriotic
Action & Adventure

Alex Ander

"There is a certain enthusiasm in liberty, that makes human nature rise above itself, in acts of bravery and heroism."

—Alexander Hamilton

Chapter 1: Cemetery

Kneeling, her butt resting on the heels of her boots, Natasha Volkov kissed her fingers and placed them on the new headstone in front of the freshly disturbed earth. "Mnogo lyubvi, papen'ka — *Much love, Papa,*" she said before standing. Natasha's mind wandered to a time from her youth when her father would put her on his lap and tell stories. Mostly, the stories were from Russian folklore, but the ones young Natasha enjoyed were those about Russian history. She had been captivated by her father's voice, telling heroic tales of czars and emperors, leading their troops into battle, defeating the enemy and saving Mother Russia from the invading hordes. Natasha smiled. To this day, she had no idea if the stories had been true, but it made no difference. The story was not important. It only served as the backdrop to spend time with her father, her Papa.

Natasha tilted her head back and let the sun's rays shine on her face. The warmth felt good. Even though the calendar showed that spring had come to Moscow, the warmer temperatures were slow to follow. It had been a brutal winter with record cold temperatures and snowfall. An overnight snowstorm had dropped a few more inches. Piles of snow still dotted the landscape, reminders of where the wind had made huge drifts over the winter. She could not remember there being a colder winter in her lifetime. She lifted the collar of her short-length fur coat around her neck and shoved her hands into the pockets.

A few minutes later, her hand vibrated. She retrieved a cell phone. Her heart beat faster. She slid her right thumb across the phone's screen and turned her head swiftly to the right to throw her long blonde hair over her shoulder. "Volkov...da — *Yes.*" She listened for a few seconds. "YA na moyem puti — *I'm on my way.*" Stowing the phone, Natasha gave her father's headstone one more look, her eyes settling on the last line: 'Predannyy Muzh i Lyubyashchiy Otets — *Devoted Husband and Loving Father.*' She did not want to leave her papa, but she had work to do.

Natasha spun around on the heels of her boots and trudged down the slope toward her waiting vehicle, her pace slow and methodic. The slope leveled off. Her mind shifted from her father to her job, and her strides grew longer and her pace quickened. With each step, the pull-tabs on her boots tapped against the metal zipper. She opened the door of her dark gray UAZ Patriot, a four-door, four-wheel drive, sport utility vehicle. Pulling up her skirt slightly, she climbed inside the SUV. Once inside, Natasha stared straight ahead. She took a deep breath and let it out. She forced herself to

7

focus on her destination, her assignment. Having left the engine of the SUV running, she put the transmission into 'drive' and sped away.

Chapter 2: Assault

The wheels of the Patriot rolled to a stop. Through the windshield, Natasha spied a house in the distance. The structure was a simple and neglected one-story residence. Smoke rose from the chimney on the far left side. A small car was parked in the driveway. The vehicle's condition matched that of the house. Getting out of her vehicle, she went to the rear and swung open the door to the luggage compartment, revealing a cache of weapons and tactical gear. She removed her coat and threw it inside before picking up a bulletproof vest. Standing, she noticed Sergei at the corner of the Patriot.

Sergei Gagarin was a member of the Spetsnaz (Special Forces) of the Federal Security Service of the Russian Federation (FSB). He was a ruggedly handsome man, although his features were hidden by the tactical gear he wore. He was three inches over six-feet tall and weighed two-hundred and twenty-five pounds. His shoulders were broad and his body was well sculpted. From behind his goggles, Sergei stared at her. His deep blue eyes met her blue eyes. He adjusted the strap attached to his SR-3M Vikhr rifle.

Natasha and Sergei had been dating for the last two years. Their relationship had been great from the beginning; however, since the death of her

9

father, they had begun arguing more. Usually, the arguments started over small matters before escalating to full-blown fights.

Last week, Natasha had told Sergei she had wanted to take some time to be alone. She needed to sort things out. The death of her father had been difficult, and she was slipping deeper and deeper into an anger-induced way of life. To make matters worse, her job was demanding more and more of her time.

Natasha was an FSB Agent, specializing in counter-terrorism, defending Russia from terrorist attacks. Over the past several months, there had been numerous assaults across the country. Citizens were terrified, never knowing when, or where, the next attack would occur. Natasha had been working overtime tracking down a serial bomber, who had exploded bombs at many locations, in and around Moscow, in the last three months. Sergei had called to inform her that a tip had come in, placing the bomber at this house. His team was in position, waiting for the order to storm the house.

"YA dumayu, chto vy dolzhny sidet' eto odin iz — *I think you should sit this one out.*" Bracing for the backlash, Sergei's muscles contracted.

Natasha glared at him. He was trying to protect her. As far as she was concerned, they were not dating anymore and her personal welfare was no longer his concern. Pointing her finger at him, she opened her mouth to speak, but stopped. Afraid of what she may say, she kept her thoughts to herself. She finished attaching the straps on her protective vest. "Bez shansov — *No chance.*" Her voice left no doubt she was angry. She picked up her SR-3M Vikhr, pulled back on the bolt and saw a round in the chamber. Releasing the bolt, she removed the magazine and made sure it was full.

Sergei did not have time to get into an argument with her that would most likely turn into a shouting match. He had a mission to complete and the other members of his team were relying on him to have his head in the game. He ogled Natasha from head to toe. "Vy deystvitel'no dumayete, chto vy odety dlya etogo — *Do you really think you're dressed for this?*" He made no effort to hide the sarcasm in his voice.

With more force than necessary, Natasha slammed the magazine into the rifle and examined her clothing. She was wearing a black bulletproof vest over a tight red knit sweater dress. The hem of the dress fell three inches above her knee. Black knee boots with chunky three-inch heels completed the outfit. She knew her clothing was not appropriate for an assault, but she had taken part in other operations and her heels and dress had been much higher.

Seeing the look on her face, Sergei made an appeal to her sensibility. "Pust' moi lyudi pnut' v dveryakh. Kogda vse yasno, mesto vse tvoye — *Let my men kick in the doors. When everything is clear, the place is all yours.*"

Natasha relented. The last thing she wanted to do was put his men at risk. She nodded her head and held out her hand, flexing her fingers. "Dayte mne naushnika — *Give me an earpiece.*" She put her rifle inside the SUV, before removing her vest and tossing it alongside the rifle.

Sergei handed her an earpiece and started jogging toward the house, two team members at his side. He gave commands over the radio. Over his shoulder, he heard Natasha call out to him.

"Byt' ostorozhen — *Be careful.*"

Sergei smiled. *Maybe not all is lost between us.*

Standing near the left-rear corner of the SUV, Natasha drew back her hair and tucked the tiny communication device into her ear. She heard Sergei's commands, while watching him and his team approach the front door. She folded her arms across her chest and rubbed the backs of her upper arms. The heels of her boots rubbed against each other, while she shifted her weight back and forth. She saw Sergei give hand signals to the men near him. The teams were preparing to breach both doors to the house, simultaneously. Natasha felt a chill run down her back. She lowered her head and realized she was standing in the cold, wearing only a dress and boots. Leaning to the right, her left foot came off the ground and the fingertips of her right hand touched the collar of her coat. Before she could close her fingers, a loud blast pierced her eardrums and the ensuing shockwave slammed into her chest like a sledgehammer.

Already off-balance, Natasha was thrown backwards several feet. She landed on her back in a spread-eagle position. Her ears ringing, she laid on the ground, staring at the sky. Particles of debris floated down around her. A hot ember, the size of a quarter, fell on her left thigh and burned a hole through her nylons. She felt nothing. It took more than a minute, but the ringing in her ears subsided. She sat up. The house was reduced to rubble. Sections of it were on fire. Black smoke rose into the air. Her senses returning, she felt searing pain in her leg. She swiped away the hot ember. There was a large hole in her nylons. The skin—usually milky white in color—was bright red. She gathered a handful of snow and held it on her thigh. She closed her eyes and sighed. A few seconds later, she opened them to the sight of the house in shambles. A teardrop ran down her cheek and her voice cracked when she whispered, "Sergei."

Minutes later, her legs began shaking and the muscles in her butt contracted. The coldness of the damp snow had seeped through her dress and nylons. Like an ocean wave, crashing against the shore, the cold ran up her body, until she was shivering from head to toe. Convulsing, she let her body fall backward. Lying on the snowy ground, she saw images of Sergei and her father flash across her mind. Fatigue set in and her eyelids drooped before closing. *I'm so tired.*

Chapter 3: Oval Office

July 8th, 8:43 a.m.; the Oval Office (the White House)

Aaron Hardy sat on the end of the couch in the Oval Office. The President of the United States, James Conklin, sat across from him in a wooden, straight back chair with leather trim. The men were discussing the details of the job the President had offered Hardy, which he accepted.

Hardy was wearing a gray suit, white shirt and a red tie. A handkerchief in his left breast pocket matched the color of his tie, which was held in place by a gold clip. A collar bar under the knot of the tie drew the points of his shirt collar closer together. The suit fit his five-feet, eleven-inch, one hundred and eighty-five-pound frame, perfectly. One week ago, he celebrated his thirtieth birthday and was in the best physical shape of his life.

Hardy had enlisted in the U.S. Marine Corps when he was eighteen years old. He spent the first four years of his career serving overseas, primarily in Iraq, before becoming a member of the Second Marine Special Operations Battalion, headquartered at Camp Lejeune, North Carolina. For the next five years, he was involved in direct-action, special reconnaissance and counter-terrorism missions, until Colonel Franklin Ludlum asked him to take command of a team and conduct top-secret missions all over the world.

One week ago, at the start of the Fourth of July holiday weekend, Hardy's teammates had been killed in an explosion at a tavern in Washington D.C. Hardy was the only survivor. During the next twenty-four hours, he tracked down those who were responsible for killing his men. With the help of Special Agent Raychel DelaCruz of the Federal Bureau of Investigation, he was able to bring the perpetrators to justice.

The President arranged a meeting with Hardy after discovering what he had done. During the meeting, the President offered Hardy a top-secret job, working directly for him. Hardy's main objective was to go on the offensive against the terrorists. Since the position did not officially exist, he would operate under special rules of engagement—his own. He would do whatever was necessary, and use whatever resources he had, to stop the terrorists before they could carry out further attacks. The President's exact words were 'to take the fight to the terrorists.'

"As I said earlier, you would have all the resources you need to get the job done." The President checked his wristwatch. "I'm sick and tired of the terrorists tying our hands and forcing us to play defense. When I campaigned for this job, I told the American people I would be tough on terror. Since taking office, I've been wrapped up in political battles that have virtually sidelined my efforts to make real progress in this war." The President shifted in his chair. "And, make no mistake, this *is* a war."

James Conklin was a man dedicated to serving the American people. He had served two terms as Governor of Massachusetts after he had returned home from serving his country. Conklin was a marine with the First Battalion 8th Marines and stationed in Beirut, Lebanon in 1983. He was among the 128 who were wounded when a suicide bomber detonated a truck bomb near the building serving as the barracks. Two-hundred forty-one American service members were killed. Conklin's hero status had helped him in his campaign for the governorship. He won in a landslide victory.

Now, at age fifty-five, he was two years into his first term. The man was in great shape for his age. His hair was gray, but showed no signs of balding. He wore a black suit with a white dress shirt. His tie was deep blue and he had a handkerchief in his left breast pocket that matched the color of his tie. Lastly, he wore a pair of black casual loafers. "Are there any—" the President started to say, but stopped when someone knocked on the door. The door to the Oval Office opened and the President's Director of the Federal Bureau of Investigation, Phillip Jameson, entered.

The President stood and glimpsed his watch. "Thanks for coming, Phil. I know you've got a lot on your plate."

"It's not a problem, sir." Jameson's long strides made short order of the distance between the door and the couch. He extended his hand toward the President, who shook it before introducing Jameson to Hardy.

"Aaron, this is my Director of the FBI, Phillip Jameson." The President faced Jameson. "Director Jameson, I want you to meet Aaron Hardy, your newest special agent. Aaron has accepted the position you and I discussed earlier, and is eager to start as soon as possible." After Jameson and Hardy had shaken hands, the President checked his watch. "Now, if you'll excuse me, gentlemen, I have a press conference in fifteen minutes." He shook Hardy's hand. "It was a pleasure meeting you, Aaron. I'm glad to have you on our team." He tipped his head toward Jameson. "You're in good hands."

"Thank you, Mr. President."

The President acknowledged Jameson. "I trust you'll fill him in on the specifics of the position as well as the details of his first mission."

"Of course I will, sir."

"Splendid," said the President, who patted Jameson on the back before heading toward the door, straightening his tie.

Jameson faced Hardy, who was already sizing up his new boss. Hardy knew Jameson had played an active role in the Fourth of July events in which Hardy was involved. He studied Jameson, taking in his demeanor and physical characteristics.

The fifty-year-old FBI Director was physically fit, regularly lifting weights and jogging. He was five-feet, eleven inches tall and weighed one hundred and ninety pounds. He was bald and wore rounded, rectangular eyeglasses with thick black frames. His work attire was always the same—black suit, white shirt, red tie. He changed the shade and print of the tie, but it was always red. His shoes were black and always polished—no smudges. His clothing was a projection of what you could expect from him. He was a man who brought to bear rock-steady leadership and decision-making skills and always backed his agents. He was also quick to get to the point.

"Let's get started." Jameson tossed a manila file folder onto the coffee table before sitting in the chair the President had vacated. "Before we go over your first mission, we need to discuss the details of your employment."

Sitting, Hardy nodded his head and leaned forward.

"Officially, your position does not exist as the President outlined it." Jameson reclined and crossed his legs. "You'll be working for the FBI and have an office in Washington D.C. Your title will reflect your cover story. You'll be acting as a consultant, advising corporations, foreign nationals, other nations...you name it...on matters pertaining to terrorism." Jameson spread his hands apart. "Keep it broad and vague when you have to discuss your credentials." He wagged his finger. "That reminds me. Here's your badge." He handed Hardy a leather bi-fold with an FBI badge and documentation with his photo and official title.

Hardy opened the leather bi-fold and read his title: Special Agent Consultant to the Director. *That's a mouthful.*

"Now, about your first mission," Jameson pointed toward the manila folder, "The details are in that file. Let's go over what you need to do."

Chapter 4: Mission

Thousands of feet above the Atlantic Ocean

Hardy sat back in his seat aboard a Gulfstream V jet, flying high above the Atlantic Ocean. He was the only passenger on the flight. The FBI used the jet to transport agents around the world. The aircraft had taken off from Washington D.C. at 1 p.m.; its destination was Moscow, Russia. After the plane had leveled off and reached its cruising speed, Hardy unbuckled his seatbelt and picked up his new phone.

He stared at the satellite phone. Even though it appeared to be exactly like any other smartphone on the market, it was a state-of-the-art piece of technology, capable of getting a communication signal where normal smartphones could not. Plus, it contained a Global Positioning System tracker that was accurate within one square block. He was not staring at the sat phone in awe of its technological advances, however. Before the Gulfstream V had taken off, Hardy made a call to Special Agent Raychel DelaCruz of the FBI. The conversation had not gone well.

Special Agent DelaCruz, her colleagues shortened her name to Cruz, had been the lead agent investigating the explosion at the tavern that killed everyone, except Hardy. His first encounter with her was at the hospital after the explosion. He had been captivated by her from the moment he opened his eyes and saw her standing over his hospital bed. Twenty-nine years old, she was both beautiful and professional. She was tall, standing five-feet, eight inches. She had dark brown hair that fell below her shoulders. Her hair was paired with an equally beautiful set of dark brown eyes. She had a long face with high cheekbones and a flawless complexion.

During the past week, Hardy and Cruz had been seeing each other, taking walks during her lunch hour and going out for drinks. Two days ago, they went out for dinner for the first time. They had a great time and made plans to go out again tonight, which made the call to her more difficult.

Hardy had told her he was going out of town, which had prompted her to ask the usual questions— where are you going?, why are you going?, how long will you be gone? Since the President had made it clear his new job was top-secret, Hardy had to tiptoe around the inquiry, unable to get into specifics. Even though she sounded like she was okay, he had sensed she was not happy with his vague responses.

Hardy closed his eyes and rested his head on the seat. He did not want to ruin what he had with her. In his line of work, it was difficult to have a serious relationship with a woman. He would be gone for long periods and he could not discuss where he had been. Since Cruz had spent long hours at her job, he had hoped she would be better able to understand his unconventional schedule. Still, no woman wanted to be separated from her man for long stretches.

He put the sat phone in his pocket and reached for the manila file folder on an adjacent seat. *I'll take her somewhere nice when I get back.* Shifting his thoughts to the mission, he opened the file and studied its contents.

Director Jameson had spent the rest of the morning briefing Hardy on the mission. It was simple in nature. He was to locate Anton Rudin, a Russian bomb maker, and kill him. Rudin was a bomb maker for hire. He made sophisticated and powerful explosive devices and sold them to anyone, or any organization, for the right price. He may not have been a terrorist, but he supplied them. The theory behind the mission was stop the bomb maker from making bombs, and the terrorists have one less resource at their disposal.

For the past five months, Russia had been experiencing a wave of domestic terrorist attacks, including several bombings in, and around, the city of Moscow. The Russian authorities suspected Rudin had supplied the bombs, but had not been able to find him. In a spirit of cooperation, Russia had contacted the White House and agreed to share the information they had on Rudin in the hopes of stopping further terrorist attacks. It was a real 'olive branch' of a gesture, since the two nations were not on the best of speaking terms.

Hardy peeled back a sheet of paper, skimmed the page beneath it and let go of the paper. The dossier of Natasha Volkov, the Russian FSB agent he was scheduled to meet in Moscow, was lengthy.

Volkov was twenty-seven years old. She had been working for the FSB for the last four years, serving in various positions. Her most recent appointment, which began shortly after the terrorist attacks had started, specialized in counter-terrorism. She was fluent in three languages, one of which was English. She graduated from Moscow State University before completing her training at the FSB Academy, where she was recognized for numerous talents, including marksmanship and criminal investigation. Hardy rubbed his eyes with his thumb and forefinger. Even though he had not met her, he could see she was an accomplished woman, at least on paper. Reading the file, he began the task of committing to memory everything the dossier contained.

Three hours later, Hardy tossed the file onto the seat. He retrieved his sat phone and checked the time before reclining in his seat. He was tired and his eyes burned. The flight to Moscow was going to take nine hours, and there was an eight-hour time difference between Washington, D.C. and the Russian capitol. He would be landing at 6 a.m., local time. He closed his eyes and relaxed. He needed to get some sleep before his 8 a.m. meeting with the FSB agent.

Chapter 5: Moscow

After the jet touched down at Moscow Domodedovo International Airport, Hardy de-boarded the aircraft, cleared the customs process and made his way to the front doors of the airport. He was to rendezvous with an American asset, who would take him to the meeting with Agent Volkov.

Outside the airport, Hardy scanned the area and spotted a man matching the description he was given. The man was tall and in his late thirties, leaning against a Volkswagen Polo Sedan, reading a newspaper. He wore a light gray suit, white shirt with a black tie and black dress shoes. On his head was a fedora-style hat, tilted backwards. Black sunglasses covered his eyes. Hardy strode toward the man. "Did the Tigers win yesterday?"

The man lowered the newspaper. "Not only did they win, but they shut out the Yankees, three to nothing."

"Myself, I'm a Lions fan."

The contact information having been verified, the man folded the newspaper and threw it into the car. He held out his hand. "I'm Tom MacPherson."

MacPherson was an American asset stationed in Moscow. He worked out of the embassy. MacPherson's American handler had contacted him and given him explicit instructions. He was to pick up Hardy at the airport, assist him during his time in the city and drop him at the airport when Hardy was finished with the mission. MacPherson was not to inquire about the nature of Hardy's visit.

The two men shook hands. "Aaron Hardy."

"Hop in." MacPherson took Hardy's suitcase and put it in the trunk of the car. He sat in the driver's seat, started the engine and navigated the sedan into traffic.

Hardy did not waste any time. "Were you able to get what I asked for?"

MacPherson tipped his head backward. "It's in the back." He was given a list of items he was to acquire for his passenger.

Hardy twisted in his seat, retrieved a duffle bag and plopped it onto his lap.

"You'll find everything you asked for is in there."

Hardy unzipped the bag and inspected the contents. "It looks good." He closed the bag and pushed it to the floor. "How far are we from the hotel?"

MacPherson scratched his chin. "About an hour, I'd say."

Hardy looked at the time on the dashboard of the car—it read 6:13. The café, where the meeting was taking place—Apartment 44—was only a few minutes away from his hotel, the Marriott. "Good. That'll give me time to get cleaned up."

For the next hour, the two men made small talk, until MacPherson brought the sedan to a stop in front of the Marriott. He popped the trunk and jumped out. Handing over Hardy's suitcase, along with a room key, MacPherson motioned toward the hotel. "You're already checked in, so you can go straight to your room.

"Thanks." Hardy accepted the items. "I'll meet you in the lobby in twenty minutes."

MacPherson nodded before getting back into the sedan and driving away.

Chapter 6: Marriott

Inside his room, Hardy started the shower and stripped, laying his clothes on the bed. He waited until the steam began to rise over the top of the shower curtain before he climbed into the stall. The hot water hit him like tiny pellets, but it felt good. He had been stuck on a plane for nine hours. After another hour in a small car, this was like a therapeutic massage. Standing with his back to the showerhead, he let the water loosen his tight muscles. He took a few extra minutes to enjoy the moist heat, before lathering and rinsing his body and hair. He rotated the shower handle to the right. Stepping out of the shower, he picked up the towel he had left on the toilet seat and wiped the remaining beads of water from his body. He tossed the towel onto the floor and left the bathroom.

Naked and standing by the bed, Hardy put on a pair of boxer shorts and blue jeans before adding a light brown t-shirt, white socks and brown hiking boot-type tennis shoes. Unzipping the duffle bag MacPherson had given him, he retrieved a Glock 19 handgun, holster, magazine pouch and two magazines. He tucked the small holster inside his waistband before attaching the clip over his belt to secure the rig. He picked up the Glock 19, retracted the slide to verify that the pistol was loaded and slid it into the holster. He put the magazine pouch on the other side of his belt and stuffed two fifteen-round magazines into it before draping his t-shirt over the gun and the magazine pouch. Slinging the duffle bag over his shoulder, he exited the hotel room.

Entering the lobby, Hardy spied MacPherson, sitting in a chair and thumbing through a magazine. Noticing Hardy, MacPherson tossed the magazine onto the table next to him and rose to his feet. The two men left and got into the sedan. Hardy put the duffle bag in the back seat.

MacPherson eased the sedan into traffic.

Hardy twirled a finger in the air. "I want to make a slow trip around the café before we park the car. Go slow, but don't make it conspicuous."

MacPherson acknowledged him.

Less than ten minutes later, the sedan turned right down a narrow side street. MacPherson pointed. "The café is up ahead on the right."

Hardy's eyes scanned the street and buildings for anything, or anyone, that seemed out of place. He did not have reason to suspect anything was going to go wrong. Being acutely aware of his surroundings was something that came natural to him; furthermore, this skill automatically kicked in whenever he was in unfamiliar territory. The street was mostly deserted. A few people mingled on the sidewalk, talking as they walked. Cars were parallel-parked on the right.

After passing the entrance to the café, MacPherson gestured. "This street dead ends up ahead. I'll have to turn around if you want to make a second pass."

"No, park up there, the last one," Hardy said, referring to the row of parallel parking spots on the right. He did not want to risk another drive past the café, in case there was someone watching.

MacPherson parked the sedan and shut off the engine. "How do you want to play this?" He removed his handgun from its holster. Pinching the slide near the muzzle between his thumb and forefinger, he pulled back the slide only enough to see a round in the chamber.

Hardy shook his head and held out his hand. "Let me see your phone."

MacPherson flicked his eyes toward the outstretched hand. "Why?"

"I'm going in alone. I want you to text me if you see anything on the street."

MacPherson relinquished his mobile.

Hardy punched in the number to his sat phone and returned the man's phone to him. After verifying his gun was loaded, he gave the street one more check before getting out of the sedan. He maintained a brisk pace toward the café, his eyes taking in every detail around him. Approaching the café, he swung open the door and stepped inside.

Chapter 7: Café

Apartment 44 was a small café. There were several round-shaped, wooden tables in the center. Matching wooden chairs with circular seats complemented the tables. Straight ahead was a dark mahogany bar. Bottles of alcohol lined a shelf behind it. A full-width mirror behind the shelf gave the illusion there were twice as many bottles. A few patrons sat at the tables. The bartender nodded at Hardy. He nodded back before choosing a table off to the side next to a large brick wall. On one side of the table were two chairs. The other side had booth seating.

Hardy sat on the booth side, his back to the wall. He placed his sat phone on the table and removed a folded newspaper from his back pocket. He placed the newspaper on the table, making sure the section heading was visible and hanging off the edge of the table. His sat phone read 7:48. He glanced around the café, noting where the exits were located.

A few minutes later, a young woman in her twenties showed up at his table, placed a menu in front of him and said something in Russian. He presumed she wanted to take his order. He tapped his finger on the rim of an empty water glass and smiled. The woman had a blank stare on her face for a split-second before she smiled back and nodded her head. She left, returned with a pitcher of water and filled the water glass. Hardy checked his sat phone again—7:55.

During the next five minutes, more patrons entered the café. Each time the door opened, Hardy observed the new arrivals. None matched the description of his contact, the FSB agent.

At eight o'clock, a woman in her mid-to-late twenties with long, blonde hair made an entrance. She stood inside the door and surveyed the people. She displayed a slender figure, five-feet, seven-inches tall, and was dressed in skin-tight blue jeans. A white short-sleeve camisole shell was tucked inside the jeans. When her eyes settled on Hardy, she paused. Dropping her cell phone into the right pocket of her black fitted knee-length blazer, she strutted toward him. Her long legs carried her across the hardwood floor with minimal steps, the hem of her blazer flaring. With each footfall, the two-inch chunky heels of her black pumps echoed in the confined space of the café. The patrons noticed her impressive entrance. They stopped their conversations and held their glasses in midair to glimpse the newcomer.

The woman stopped at Hardy's table. She put her right hand on the back of the nearest chair and eyed the newspaper. The section heading, 'sports,' was hanging off the edge of the table. "My money is on the Yankees this year."

Now that she was standing in front of him, Hardy saw her beauty. Her skin was white, almost like cream. Her blue eyes were set above a narrow nose and below impeccably manicured eyebrows. When she spoke, her full lips parted and revealed a set of white teeth, brilliant in color and perfectly aligned. Her photo in the dossier did not do her justice.

"They'll never make it past Boston."

"Boston's bullpen is terrible."

Hardy stood and extended his hand. "I'm Aaron Hardy."

She shook his hand. "Natasha Volkov—it's a pleasure to meet you, Mr. Hardy." She slid the chair out from under the table and sat.

"Likewise, Ms. Volkov." He took his seat.

"Please call me Natasha. I find Ms. Volkov a bit too...*old*...for my tastes." She smiled and half-chuckled. "Perhaps if we meet again in forty years, you can call me, Ms. Volkov."

Hardy laughed as the young woman, who had brought him his water, spoke to Natasha. Natasha replied, and the woman left and came back with a pitcher of water and filled Natasha's water glass.

After the woman had left, Natasha directed her attention toward Hardy. *He's handsome.* She eyed his facial features. He had light brown hair, cut short. His jaw was square. His chin came to a slight point and had a tiny dimple in the center. She was drawn to his deep blue eyes. They made her feel as if he was peering into her inner being. His physique was muscular. His biceps stretched the sleeves of his brown t-shirt to the point where she was expecting the fabric to split at the seam.

She had always been intrigued by American men. They seemed to be freer and more relaxed than their Russian counterparts were, but every bit as tough. Inwardly, she laughed. Maybe she had seen too many American movies when she was younger. "My superiors tell me we're to work together."

Hardy detected a sarcastic tone in her voice, but dismissed it.

She opened the menu and pretended to be deciding on what to order. "So, let's work together. You can start by telling me what you know about Anton Rudin."

Hardy did not appreciate this woman's attitude; however, in this scenario, he was the visiting team and he wanted to get off to a good start. He opened the folded newspaper, took out a few documents and a map of a specific location in Russia. He placed everything in front of him. "A couple of weeks ago, the FBI uncovered and stopped a plot to blow up the Golden Gate Bridge during rush hour traffic. During the investigation, they captured the man who was going to set off the explosion. He had entered the United States from Russia, one week earlier."

Natasha closed the menu and set it aside.

Hardy took a drink of water. "Fast forwarding a little...during the interrogation, the FBI discovered the identity of the man who was to *make* the bomb that was going to be used on the bridge."

Natasha crossed her legs and leaned forward in her chair. "Anton Rudin?"

Hardy nodded. "The man in custody divulged the location of where he had met Rudin when he was in Russia." Hardy twisted the map and pointed to a location and the address of the house where the

33

man had met Rudin. "My people believe this is the best place to begin our search for Rudin." Hardy slid the other documents across the table.

Natasha peered at the map and recognized the address. Without realizing what she was doing, she reached under the table and rubbed the top of her left thigh. She stared at the map in silence. Images of Sergei flashed across her mind. Even though it was not on the map, she envisioned the house, the explosion, the debris. The entire incident came rushing back to her.

Hardy thought she was inspecting the map, but when several awkward moments had passed, he knew something was wrong. "What's the matter?" She did not respond. Reaching out, he touched the map. "Natasha?" She flinched. "Are you okay?"

She blinked several times and took a drink of water. "I'm fine." Her eyes went back to the map. "No, there's nothing there. My people have already—" she paused before flatly stating, "There's nothing there."

"I'd still like to see the house. Maybe, something was overlooked. It can't hurt to have another pair of eyes—"

Natasha cut him off in mid-sentence. "Trust me." Her voice grew louder with each successive word. "There's *nothing* there."

Hardy had touched a nerve. He wanted to push her on the issue. The FBI had been certain there was a better than good chance Rudin used the house as a home base. After staring at her for several moments, he decided not to push it. He remained quiet, letting her read the rest of the documents.

Natasha held a sheet of paper in the air, while she read the next. She consumed everything Hardy and the Americans had on Anton Rudin. She frowned and her eyebrows curled downward. The Americans had no new information. She tightened her grip on the papers, crinkling them. Her government had insisted she work with Hardy in the spirit of cooperation to find Rudin. *Why?* It was obvious the Americans had nothing of value to offer. She put the papers in order and passed them back across the table.

Hardy wasted no time in quizzing her. "Now, it's your turn. What information do you have?" He took the papers and set them on the folded newspaper.

Natasha studied Hardy for several seconds. After taking a drink of water, she glanced over her shoulder. "Look, my government has ordered me to work with you. Why, I don't know. Your country has nothing new to offer in this matter; however," she tugged on the lapels of her jacket to straighten it, "in the spirit of cooperation, I will play nice." She smiled at Hardy, but did a poor job disguising her feelings. "I'm this close," she lifted her hand, her thumb and forefinger close together, "to finding Rudin. I'm waiting for a call from one of my contacts. He thinks he knows where Rudin is hiding." Natasha stood, the backs of her knees pushing the chair away from the table. "Where are you staying?"

"The Marriott," replied Hardy. *She's going to blow me off.*

"Good. Go back to your hotel and rest. When I find out more, I'll call you." She spun around, "I'll be in touch, Mr. Hardy," and marched toward the door.

Hardy watched her leave, his hand shaking from the death grip on the water glass. She had dismissed him with a virtual 'don't call me, I'll call you' attitude. She had not given him any information. This meeting had been a disaster. *So much for cooperation.* Still fuming, he considered his options; go after her and insist on being involved in the conversation with her contact, follow her or visit the site on the map himself. He was contemplating a fourth option when he noticed something odd on the other side of the café.

Chapter 8: Surprised

Natasha left the café. She had no plans to contact
Hardy when she found Rudin. She had worked
hard, tracking the man to that dilapidated house,
only to have him slip though her fingers. Sergei's
death would not be in vain. No, when she found
Rudin, she was going to be the one who brought him
to justice. No pretty boy American was going to take
from her the satisfaction owed. After Rudin was in
custody, she would call Hardy and give him an
excuse for why she had not called him sooner. *It was
a matter of urgency and I needed to move fast. That
should placate him.*

Reaching the sidewalk, she heard her phone
ring. It was her contact. She swiped a finger across
the screen before tucking the phone under her hair.
"Tell me you found him." Focusing on the voice on
the other end of the phone, she listened.

Striding up the sidewalk of the narrow, deserted
street, she was paying too much attention to the
caller and did not see the slow-moving black van to
the right, until it was too late.

The van accelerated and came alongside Natasha
before swerving left and coming to a halt, the tires
screeching. The side doors were open. Two men
jumped out and rushed her. She dropped her
phone, threw back the right lapel of her open-front

blazer. Before she could get to her weapon, the first man latched on to her right arm and twisted it behind her back. The second man took her pistol from her holster. The first man, who still held her arm behind her back, grabbed a handful of hair, took two steps toward the van and threw Natasha through the open doors.

She threw out her left hand to break her fall, her palm skidding across the rough fibers of the van's carpeted floor. She landed on her stomach, her knees hitting the metal trim of the van's running boards. The surge of adrenaline kept any pain from reaching her brain. She rolled onto her left side and brought her right foot up, ready to drive the heel of her shoe into the first target presented. She lined up her foot with the center of the man's chest, the one who had thrown her into the van. She never got the chance to deliver her strike, however.

As the men approached the van, Natasha heard several loud bangs. The men's shirts split open in several different spots. The second man staggered backward and hit the open door of the van before sliding to the pavement. The first man dropped to his knees, his upper body landing inside the van. Staring at Natasha, he appeared to have been shot. She was not going to be denied her revenge, however. She thrust her leg toward the man, the heel of her shoe landing squarely on the man's nose. After a loud crack, streams of blood stained the carpet. His head rocked backward and he disappeared from sight. Before she could get to her feet, she noticed movement to the right.

Chapter 9: Newspaper

Hardy followed a man from the café. The man had sat in the corner, pretending to read a newspaper. Hardy had noticed the man never flipped a single page of the newspaper. Occasionally, he would peer over the paper, looking at Natasha. After she had gone, the man chucked the newspaper, tossed a few Rubles on the table and left.

On the street, Hardy saw the scene unfold. The van came to a quick stop, blocking Natasha's forward movement. Two men jumped out, rushing toward her. Watching them throw her through the side doors, Hardy knew what was coming next and he had to act. Drawing his Glock 19, he took a step to the right to get a clear shot at the two men near the van. He pressed the pistol's trigger several times, shooting the man to the left four times, hitting him in the torso. The last shot penetrated his ear, sending him crumpling to the concrete. Transitioning to the second man, Hardy shot him multiple times, until he fell through the van's open doors. The man from the café telegraphed a move for a holstered weapon. Hardy had been waiting to see what the man would do. He had to make sure the newcomer was not coming to Natasha's aid. When Hardy saw the pistol on the man's hip, he had seen enough. He put his pistol's front sight on the man's nose and pulled back on the trigger. Mr. Newspaper collapsed into a heap, never getting the chance to draw the pistol.

Hardy sprinted toward the van. Keeping a safe distance from the open doors, he swung his pistol around and pointed it inside. Natasha was on the floor, a man squatting behind her and pressing the muzzle of a gun against her right temple. His other arm had her in a headlock. She was off-balance, unable to fight back.

The man said something to Hardy in Russian and drove the muzzle deeper into her skin. Natasha's eyes squinted and she groaned. Her windpipe was being crushed. Hardy leveled the Glock at the man's right eye. "I'm sorry, but I don't speak Russian."

Again, the man spoke to Hardy in his native language.

Not taking his eyes off his adversary, Hardy spoke to Natasha. "Natasha, this ugly oaf doesn't know what I'm saying, so this is what's going to happen." Hardy waited again to see if his comment got any reaction from the man. It did not. "When I count to three, you're going to tilt your head to *your* left as far as you can. Understand?"

Struggling against her captor's grasp, Natasha held her hands in front of her, her eyes wide. She managed to shake her head, no.

"Trust me, Natasha. You're not the only one who graduated at the top of the class in marksmanship. On three, tilt your head to your left." Hardy gripped his Glock a little tighter. "One."

Natasha's adrenaline coursed through her body. Her heart pounded in her chest and she could feel her pulse throbbing in her temples.

"Two."

Natasha had met Hardy less than thirty minutes ago. He was expecting her to place her life in his hands. She was not a religious person, but she said a quick prayer and lowered her hands, hearing Hardy say the next number.

"Three!"

Natasha put all of the adrenaline surging through her veins to good use. She yanked her head to the left as hard as she could. The muscles on the right side of her neck burned. She thought if she did not die from a gunshot wound to the head, she would break her neck.

Hardy had noticed the gun being held to Natasha's head was a Sig Sauer, a double-action/single-action pistol. The hammer was forward and in double-action mode. The man's trigger finger would have to travel further and exert more energy to discharge the gun. Hardy took advantage of those factors.

He applied steady pressure to the trigger of his Glock. Natasha had jerked her head far enough to give him a clear shot. He only needed one. The gun in his hands roared. The muzzle rose and fell.

The muzzle of Hardy's pistol settled and he saw the man's body go limp. The grasp around Natasha's neck loosened and the arm slid off her shoulder. The arm holding the Sig Sauer dropped to the floor of the van. The man's body slowly leaned back and came to rest against the unopened door of the van.

Natasha rolled to her left, clutching her neck and coughing. In between coughs, she shouted at Hardy, using her native tongue.

An interpreter was not necessary. He had learned a few Russian words, starting with the curse words she was spewing. She was not was angry. Adrenaline and fear were driving her emotions.

Hardy started searching the dead men, while Natasha regained her senses. The first man had a badge. He was a member of law enforcement. Hardy felt a lump form in his throat. He had killed a cop. He held the badge, so Natasha could see it.

Climbing out of the van, she retrieved her handgun from the ground and holstered it. She snatched the badge from Hardy's hand and examined it. "What the hell?" she said. Her voice was deeper and hoarse. She held the shield she carried on a daily basis. *They're FSB?*

Hardy checked the other bodies. Each one had the same badge.

Natasha rubbed her throat. "I don't understand this."

Hearing the gunshots, MacPherson came running from the parked sedan, surprising Natasha, who spun and reached for her gun.

Hardy stopped her. "It's all right. He's with me." He pointed at the dead men. "Are these friends of yours?"

Moving from one to the next, she examined each of their faces. "I've never seen them before, but that doesn't mean anything. The FSB is a large agency with many, many agents in its employ."

"What happened," asked MacPherson, holstering his gun?

Hardy gestured at the corpses. "They tried to kidnap Natash...Agent Volkov." Without formality, Hardy introduced them to each other. "Agent Volkov...MacPherson...MacPherson...Agent Volkov."

MacPherson said, "Pleasure."

Not making eye contact, she replied, "Pleasure."

Natasha reached into her pocket. "I've got to call this in." Not finding her phone, she jerked her head left and right. The cell was lying on the ground where the man had grabbed her arm. She picked up the device and brushed off the dirt.

"Wait a minute." Hardy held up his hand. "Are you sure you want to do that?"

"I have to. I'm an FSB agent. I have to report this." She tapped the screen, dialing the number for her supervisor.

"Exactly. These are *your people*. Why would they want to abduct you? That makes no sense."

She stopped dialing and looked at him.

"You don't know who you can trust. You don't know who ordered this."

In the distance, wailing sirens grew louder. MacPherson joined the conversation. "In a few minutes, this area is going to be crawling with police. Whatever you plan on doing, you need to do it, *now*."

Hardy saw patrons from the café, peeking out the window. Some were making their way outside to see the commotion. "He's right. We need to leave."

Natasha held out her arms. "And, go where? We don't know what's going on here. I need to find out who these people are and what they wanted from me." She coughed before massaging her throat.

"You're not going to find answers if you're arrested by the police. Instead, you'll be answering *their* questions."

Natasha stared at the dead bodies. He was right. Without more information, the police would assume she and Hardy were guilty of killing four FSB agents. She slid her phone into her blazer pocket. "All right, let's go." She hurried up the sidewalk. "My vehicle is right around the corner."

Hardy waved off MacPherson. "Get out of here. I'll find my way home, somehow. Thanks for your help."

MacPherson nodded. "Take care, Hardy."

Hardy ran to catch up with Natasha at the corner of the main cross street. Her SUV was a few parking spaces away. After they got into the vehicle, she brought the engine to life, peeled away from the curb and accelerated as fast as she could without drawing attention.

Chapter 10: Roadside

Once they were a safe distance away from the scene behind them, Natasha stopped the Patriot on the side of a deserted road. She slammed the gear selector into 'park' and leaned back, running her fingers through her hair before interlocking them behind her head. She mulled over the incident outside the café. *Could my own people be responsible? They were definitely FSB agents. Their badges seemed real enough.* Letting her arms fall, her hands smacked against her thighs. She let out a long breath and her bangs shot upward.

Hardy knew what she was feeling—betrayal. Recently, he had faced a similar situation. He gave her a few minutes before pressing her. "What are we going to do, Natasha?" He would have loved to take charge, but he was in uncharted waters. The mission had taken a left turn.

She rolled her eyes toward him. Her head followed. *That's a good question.* She had been attacked by her fellow agents and was essentially on the run from the police. Staring at Hardy, her thoughts lingered over whether she could trust him.

"Who knew about your meeting with me?"

Natasha thought for a moment. "I was ordered to work with you by my boss, the director of the FSB." She paused. "There were several other agents who knew about it." She stared out the window. The sun was rising and the day was getting warmer. "Anyone could have known about it. It wasn't exactly a secret."

"So, you can't trust anybody in your agency. Everyone's a suspect. It looks like it's up to us to find out what's going on." Moments of silence passed, while they pondered their options. "Again, what are we going to do? What's our next move, Natasha?" He was in a foreign country and did not have any sources to contact, a position with which he was unfamiliar. Like it or not, he was reliant on his new 'partner.'

Hardy's words, 'you can't trust anybody in your agency,' echoed in her mind. Calling the police would likely result in her arrest and a possible murder charge. No, contact with her agency was off the table. Someone there wanted her out of the way. She was confident this attack was related to her search for Rudin. She had focused most of her resources on capturing him. In fact, during the last three months, every other case on her list had been sidelined. To find out who was behind this attack, she would have to catch Rudin and squeeze him for information. Natasha glimpsed Hardy out of the corner of her eye. Reluctantly, she would have to confide in him. Unfortunately, the next phase in their working relationship was about to begin on a sour note, the revelation of a lie.

Natasha studied her fingernails. She picked at one and flicked her fingers.

"Natasha?"

She waited until the silence became more unbearable than the truth. Whipping her head away from him, she came clean. "I was on the phone with my contact," she spoke as if reading from a script, "when those men attacked me. He told me where I could find Rudin." Staring at the floor, she felt his eyes, penetrating to her core.

"You weren't going to tell me about it, were you?"

She rubbed the palm of her left hand, the hand that had saved her face from skidding across the floor of the van.

"You were going to give me a courtesy call...*after* you had already picked him up." Hardy's pulse beat faster and the muscles in his jaw tightened. "If this is what *you people* consider cooperation, then I don't want any part of it. It's no wonder diplomatic relations between our two countries have soured. You people—"

Natasha whipped her head toward him. Fire burned in her eyes. "And, what is *your* angle in all of this? I'm sure you and your country aren't solely interested in helping us find a bomb maker devastating my people *out of the kindness of your heart*. What's the *real* reason you're here, Hardy? Can you tell me...without using the word 'cooperation' in the sentence?"

"I'm here to end Rudin's life. He's a bomb maker, who sells to the highest bidder. I take him out and he can't make any more bombs. It's that simple. There's no angle other than I want to see him dead."

"Oh, if it were only that simple. But it seldom is, though. You Americans look out for your own interests. You intervene in the affairs of other nations to accumulate wealth and power, influencing those nations to do your bidding. You're a selfish and self-centered people. You think you are the greatest nation to grace the face of the earth." Natasha looked up and raised her hands—"God's gift to the human race." She shook her head. "You people are so arrogant." She started to turn away, but stopped and jabbed a finger in his Hardy's direction. "Believe me when I tell you...your American Influence does not hold the power you *think* it does with my country."

Hardy and Natasha sat in silence for several minutes. She gripped the steering wheel hard enough to turn her knuckles white. Resting on his legs, Hardy's fists were clenched. Afraid of what they may say if the conversation continued, the agents remained quiet.

Natasha had lost much in a short time. She had not recovered from her father's death when Sergei was killed less than a month later. Her nerves were raw. Lately, she had lashed out at anyone who crossed her, even over trivial matters. She glimpsed Hardy out of the corner of her eye. If their working arrangement had any chance of succeeding, she was going to have to temper her feelings. *Maybe, he has no ulterior motive in this. We need to start over...if that's possible.*

Natasha released her grip on the steering wheel and flexed her fingers. She twisted in her seat to face

48

him, making a mental note to soften the tone of her voice. "I know this may seem odd, coming at a time like this, but I never got a chance to thank you for saving my life back there. Thank you." She let her words hang in the air. "What made you come after me?"

Hardy gritted his teeth. Oddly, he had been asking himself the same question. Risking his life to save a woman, who repaid him with insults to his integrity—and his country—had not been part of the plan. If he had stayed seated in the café and not followed that man...he let his thoughts trail off before reprimanding himself. *You're not that kind of man.* He had done the right thing. Unclenching his fists and wiggling his fingers, Hardy made a conscious effort to relax his chest muscles.

He shot a look out the window. "There was a man in the café," Hardy's voice was matter-of-factly, "who pretended to be reading a newspaper. He left right after you did. I followed him and saw the whole thing." He faced her and struggled to add a touch of warmth to his tone. "You're welcome. I'm glad I was there."

Natasha noted his exaggerated attempt at a pleasantry; however, she felt an undertone of sincerity in his words. Like her, he was trying. *Yes, I think I might be able to trust him.* After those words entered her mind, she inwardly laughed. Hardy had killed four men to save her. If it were not for his actions, she would have been abducted, possibly dead by now. "Go after him."

Hardy's eyebrows furled downward. "What are you talking about?"

"You asked me, 'what are we going to do?' We know where Rudin is hiding. Let's go after him. That's why you're here, isn't it? That's why we're working together. And, I'm thinking he might have some answers about those FSB agents back there. What is it that you Americans say?" She paused a moment, thinking of the phrase. "It's a win-win." She cocked her head to the left and raised her eyebrows, hoping the idiom would lighten the mood.

Natasha's attempt at humor was lost on Hardy. His mind was elsewhere. Killing Rudin was the purpose of his mission. In order to accomplish that, he and Natasha needed to be on the same side. She had made an effort to make amends for her words—and actions. *A fresh start.* He nodded. "Where is he?"

A smile formed on Natasha's face. She took out her cell phone. "East of St. Petersburg, on the outskirts of town," she replied, touching her phone's screen. "My source told me he has armed men with him. So, we're going to need some help."

"Who are you calling?"

She hesitated and shot him a sideways glance. "Some friends of mine from the FSB..."

Hardy rolled his eyes.

"They can help."

"We've been over this. You don't know who's responsible for sending those men."

Natasha put the mobile to her ear. "Yes, but I know these men and they would do anything for me. I trust them with my life."

"I hope you're right, because it's not just *your* life on the line."

Natasha put her hand on his forearm. "I put my life in *your* hands in that van. Now, it's time to repay that faith."

Hardy glanced at her hand. Trust was a complicated issue. He was accustomed to being in control of missions and situations. He gave the orders and his men followed, trusting in *his* judgment.

Natasha patted his arm and smiled. A second later, the familiar, deep voice of a man she knew and respected sounded in her ear. "Victor, it's Natasha." She turned away from Hardy.

"Natasha," Victor's smile came through the line, "it's good to hear your voice. How are you?"

"I'm doing well, Victor, but I need your help."

"What is it?"

"How soon can you get your team ready for a trip to St. Petersburg?"

"Not long, why? What's going on?"

She took her phone away from her ear and tapped the screen several times. "I just sent you the address of the location. I need to find someone there and the people inside will not be receptive to a knock on the door. I'll explain when you get there."

"I'll send you a text when I know our ETA."

"Thanks, Victor." Natasha eyed Hardy. "Oh, I'll be coming to the event, *plus one*. Is there any chance you can bring a grab bag?"

"I'll see what I can do."

Natasha ended the call and stashed the phone. Not having shut off the Patriot's engine, she lowered the gearshift into 'drive' and re-entered the roadway. Not taking her eyes off the road, she addressed her passenger. "Settle in, we've got a long drive ahead of us. If the traffic isn't too bad, we can make it in less than nine hours."

Hardy checked his sat phone—8:37. Not looking forward to another nine hours in confined quarters, he reached between his legs and found the lever to move the seat back. Realizing it was already back as far as it could go, he groaned under his breath.

"Are you hungry?"

"I'm starving." He had eaten a bagel and cream cheese on the flight, but that was not nearly enough food.

"I know a place on the way. It's about an hour from here. We can get something there."

Chapter 11: Rudin

Anton Rudin sat on a stool, hunched over an old wooden farm table that had seen many family dinners throughout the decades. Children would have gathered at the table, eager to see what their mother had prepared. Never in their wildest dreams would past occupants of the house have imagined the table holding the items it now held.

Rudin pushed the bridge of his gold round eyeglasses further up his long, pointed ski-slope-shaped nose. Beads of sweat dotted his forehead. His black hair was cut short and parted on the side. He was a small man, barely five-and-a-half-feet tall, and had a thin build. Fortunately, his skills did not require him to use his brawn. No, he made his living with his mind.

Rudin finished wiring the remote detonator to the last of four bombs. His cell phone on the table vibrated. He leaned over and sighed. It was his current employer. The man had hired him to make the four bombs. The man had also hired him to make, place and detonate the bombs that had exploded in Moscow over the last six months. Rudin did not see himself as a terrorist. In his mind, he was a businessperson, a supplier. It was a simple issue of supply and demand. There was a need for what he made and he filled that need. The man he was about to talk to, however, had wanted Rudin to be more than a supplier.

Rudin despised the client, but the man paid very well for the bomb maker's services. Once these four devices were in place, Rudin would receive the final installment. The money would be enough to allow him to live comfortably for the rest of his life, which was going to be a long time, since he was only forty-five years old. He had made plans to use his newfound wealth to leave Russia. He hated the cold winters, and the older he got, the more his body protested. He had his eyes set on somewhere warm, somewhere tropical. A place with beautiful sunsets and miles and miles of coastline, speckled with pretty girls in skimpy bikinis. Rudin smiled, envisioning the scene.

Letting go of the pliers, he grabbed the mobile. "Da — *Yes.*"

"Gotovy li oni yeshche — *Are they ready yet?*" asked the man.

"YA tol'ko chto zakonchil — *I just finished,*" replied Rudin.

"Khorosho. Grafik byl peremeshchen vverkh. Vy dolzhny poluchit' ikh na meste v nastoyashcheye vremya. Moi lyudi vstretyat vas v tochke sblizheniya. K tomu vremeni, vy poluchayete k mestu, bezopasnost' budut udaleny, i u vas ne budet nikakikh poluchat' cherez vorota. — *Good. The timetable has been moved up. You need to get them in place, now. My men will meet you at the rendezvous point. By the time you get to the location, security will be removed and you'll have no trouble getting through the gate."*

"Chto mozhno skazat' o zhenshchine iz FSB? Ona stanovitsya vse blizhe i blizhe — *What about the woman from the FSB? She is getting closer and closer."*

"Ne bespokoytes' o ney. Ya dogovorilsya. Ona budet zabotit'sya — *Don't worry about her. I've made arrangements. She will be taken care of."* The man paused and added, "Ne vint eto vverkh. Vy budete shchedro zaplatili, no tol'ko yesli vam eto udastsya. Otkaz ne budet dopuskat'sya — *Don't screw this up. You'll be paid generously, but only if you succeed. Failure will not be tolerated."* As soon as the man had finished speaking, he hung up the phone, not giving Rudin a chance to respond.

Setting the cell on the table, Rudin began giving orders to the men. One of them, holding a spatula in his hand, tossed things into a plastic garbage bag, while another gathered large pieces of paper on a nearby table. Rudin screamed, "Ostav'te vse. My dolzhny idti! — *Leave everything. We have to go now!"*

Chapter 12: Popovich

General Popovich hung up the phone and leaned back in his chair. He swiped the tip of a wooden match across the matchbox. Sparks flew and a small flame grew. He brought the match to the cigar he was biting. After a few puffs, he shook the match and tossed it—and the matchbox—onto his desk. He put his feet up, his combat boots landing on the desk near a coffee cup. The surface of the black liquid inside vibrated. Thick smoke from the cigar hung in the air above his head.

General Popovich was fifty-seven years old. His gray hair had receded to the top of his head. A thick, gray mustache covered his upper lip. Above the lip was a large and bulbous nose, heavily pockmarked. His dark eyes were deeply set. Bushy eyebrows hung over them, almost coming together to form one brow. He was of average height, but he had gained much weight in the last ten years. His neck spilled over the collar of his uniform, while the buttons strained to keep the lapels together.

General Popovich was the head of the Premier's security team. Prior to accepting the job, he had been a high-ranking member of the KGB, Russia's intelligence agency, until its breakup in 1991. He continued to serve in the intelligence arena as an FSB agent, until his departure five years ago. Two years ago, the Premier had asked him to come out of retirement and lead the Premier's security team.

The General was a hardliner. He longed for the old days, when Russia was a superpower. His country had been feared and respected by other nations. Its citizens had been proud and could hold their heads high.

Russia had become weak, however. Western culture had invaded its borders, bringing with it decadence and decay. Young people wanted freedom, chanting in the streets, protesting against the government. Using technology, they took to the Internet to broadcast their message to others like them. What those fools did not understand was that freedom was not free. Freedom came at the cost of security. But, those immature idealists thought they could have both. Popovich needed to change their way of thinking before beautiful Mother Russia was lost forever.

General Popovich took the cigar from his mouth and tapped it on the lip of the ashtray. He returned the cigar to his mouth, clasped his thick, pudgy fingers together and put his hands behind his head. Plans had been set in motion that would bring about the change his country required. The Russian people were already living in a state of fear, teetering on the brink of surrender. Popovich's next move would show his fellow citizens that no one was safe from terror. The only thing that would save them was to give the government more power and more control. In this way, Russia would become great again.

Chapter 13: Farmhouse

5:16 p.m.; thirty-five minutes southeast of St. Petersburg, Russia

At one time, the old single-story farmhouse would have been attractive. Centered on several acres of rich farmland, the house would have sheltered families from the brutal Russian winters, while the land would have provided food. The dwelling was situated at the base of a sloping hill. There was a grove of trees at the top of the hill; oaks and pines, among others, standing guard for more than a century.

The structure was in a state of disrepair. The chimney was missing so many bricks that light passed through it. The wooden siding was rotted and many pieces had been blown away. Even the wraparound porch had not escaped the effects of the elements. The handrail was loose; large sections were missing. The floorboards were in place, but they were splintered and rough. Having long been abandoned, the farmhouse had stood its ground in silence, until three days ago when several men showed up.

On the other side of the hill, just past the stand of trees, a small SUV was parked near the edge of the tree line. Natasha gazed through the windshield of her Patriot. "The house is just over that hill." She checked the time on her cell phone. "Victor will be here soon." Exiting the SUV, she closed the door and climbed into the backseat. Once the door was shut, she drove her knees into the seat cushion and leaned into the luggage compartment.

With her back to him, Hardy saw her hauling items from the compartment and tossing them onto the seat; some fell onto the floor. He looked closer and noticed a bulletproof vest, a pair of black tactical pants and a pair of six-inch boots. He did not recognize the name on the items—everything was in Russian—but he could see they were of similar quality to the gear he used. Hardy flicked his eyes to the right; they opened wider.

Still on her knees and facing away from him, Natasha had removed her long blazer, kicked off her shoes and pushed her jeans to her knees. Only a couple of feet away from Hardy's face, a pair of white lace-trimmed bikini underwear separated him from her butt. She spun around, plopped onto the seat and wiggled out of the jeans. Out of the corner of her eye, she saw Hardy whip his head away from her.

Sitting on the seat, wearing only her underwear and a short sleeve camisole, she smiled and realized he must have gotten an eyeful. Her mind had been so focused on getting into her tactical clothing she had forgotten there was another person in the vehicle. She buttoned her pants and shirt. "It's all right. We're both adults. I don't have anything you haven't already seen."

"I'm sorry. I was just admiring your," Hardy shut his eyes and winced—*bad choice of words*—"looking at your tactical gear."

Pulling on her boots and slipping into the bulletproof vest, she grinned. "*Tactical gear*, huh? Is that what a butt's called in America? Is that slang?" She grabbed her SR-3M Vikhr rifle and placed it on the floor. "I'm dressed now."

Pivoting in the seat, his cheeks crimson, Hardy saw the playful grin on Natasha's face. "You know what I meant." The awkward situation had morphed into a moment of lightheartedness. It was good to see this woman had a sense of humor. He pointed at her with his chin. "I think I'm a bit underdressed for the occasion."

Wearing full tactical clothing from head to toe, including a bulletproof vest, Natasha removed the magazine from the weapon, checked to make sure it was full and re-inserted it. She pulled back on rifle's bolt and saw a round in the chamber. Hearing a vehicle behind her, she glanced over her shoulder. A black SUV had rolled up to the right of the Patriot. Opening the door, she got out and leaned back inside. "Not for much longer. Come on."

Hardy stepped out of the vehicle and stretched his arms before putting his hands on his lower back and bending side to side. He watched three large men exit the black SUV. Dressed similar to Natasha, each of the men greeted her with a broad smile, kissed her on each cheek and proceeded to talk to her in Russian. Even though Hardy could not understand what they were saying, he could tell from the facial expressions that Natasha meant a great deal to these men. Hardy waited patiently for them to finish their reunion. One of the men, the tallest and oldest of the three, stopped talking and noticed Hardy. The other two men followed suit. Natasha made the introductions.

"This is Aaron Hardy. He's assisting me in tracking down Rudin." She pointed to the man furthest away from her. "Aaron, meet Nikolai Pushkin and Ivan Strovsky. They don't speak any English." Both men were similar in appearance; short blonde hair, square jaw, six-feet, two inches tall and weighing at least two hundred and twenty pounds. The only discerning feature between them was Nikolai's cleft chin. Both men nodded their heads and shook Hardy's hand.

"And, this big ox is Victor." She put her hand on the man's shoulder, which was almost higher than the top of her head. Victor Yedemsky smiled at Natasha before stepping forward and extending his hand toward Hardy.

Victor was easily six-feet, five inches in height and weighed thirty pounds more than either Nikolai or Ivan. Victor had dark hair, cut short, but not in a military-style crew cut. His green eyes were set far apart, beneath his sparse eyebrows. A well-manicured mustache rested below a wide nose with flaring nostrils. Even though he was in his mid-forties, his skin was weathered and displayed light pockmarks, especially the cheeks.

All members of the Russian Spetsnaz knew the name, Victor Yedemsky. He was a living legend in the Spetsnaz community. During his twenty years of service, he had seen action in many of the terrorist attacks that had taken place in his country, including the Moscow Theater Hostage Crisis in October 2002. In that incident, 40 terrorists took 916 guests hostage. The three-day standoff ended when security forces, which Victor was among, stormed the theater and stopped the terrorists from triggering bombs that would have brought down the building.

Victor had also been assigned to combat the worst act of terrorism in Russian history, the September 2004 hostage crisis at a school in Beslan, North Ossentia. One thousand, one hundred, twenty-eight people were taken hostage; 333 of them were killed, including 186 children. That had been a difficult day for Victor. Months later, he was still mentally recovering from Beslan. To this day, images from that attack haunt him in his sleep.

"It's nice to meet you, Mr. Hardy." Victor had a strong Russian accent.

Hardy shook Victor's hand, feeling the strength of the man's grip. "The pleasure is mine."

"Come," said Victor. "I have something for you." Everyone moved to the back of the black SUV. Victor opened the back door, dragged a duffle bag closer and unzipped it. "I think they'll fit." Inside the bag was the exact same black tactical clothing all of them were wearing, including a bulletproof vest, helmet and goggles. "Finally, this is for you, too." He picked up the same type of rifle that Natasha had been holding earlier and handed it to Hardy. "If you need a crash course in operating it, Nikolai or Ivan can help with that."

"Thanks, but I've handled one before." Hardy dropped the magazine, slid the bolt back and forth a few times, re-inserted the magazine and operated the bolt to chamber a round.

Victor was impressed. Not many people outside of Russia were familiar with a Vikhr. "Very good," he said, before pointing toward the hill and giving his men instructions. The two men checked their weapons and took off toward the hill, each in a different direction. When they had gone, he turned back to Natasha. "I heard you were involved in a shooting in Moscow that killed four FSB agents. Is that true?"

Natasha glanced at Hardy, who was in the process of emptying the duffle bag. He stopped and the two of them exchanged glances.

Victor's eyes shifted from Natasha to Hardy before coming back to Natasha. He saw the body language. "It's true, isn't it?"

"Yes," said Natasha, who described the incident at the café.

Victor put his hand on her shoulder. After she had recanted the story, he faced Hardy, who was buttoning the black shirt. He put his meaty hands on Hardy, one on each shoulder.

Hardy's muscles contracted and he clenched his fists, a kneejerk reaction.

Victor drew Hardy closer and kissed him, once on each cheek. "Thank you, Mr. Hardy, for saving Natasha's life. I am in your debt, sir."

Hardy relaxed. He thought he was going to have to fight this mountain of a man. He smiled. "We can start by dropping the 'sir' and 'mister.' Call me, Hardy."

Victor smiled and slapped Hardy on the back.

Hardy showed no emotion, but Victor's slap reminded Hardy of his high school days, specifically, being hit with a wet towel in the locker room. *That's going to leave a mark.*

Hardy put on the rest of the tactical clothing. The shirt and pants were a good fit, but the boots were too big. He opted to wear his own boots. He gazed at Victor and Natasha. They had walked several feet away and were talking in Russian. The discussion grew more intense. Natasha was animated, moving her hands and arms, while Victor remained calm. Her behavior was similar to when she was upset with Hardy back in Moscow. There was one major difference, though. At this moment, she was twice as upset. Hardy finished attaching the straps on his bulletproof vest before joining them.

Re-positioning the vest to get more comfortable, he stood next to the Russians. "Is everything okay?"

"What do you think?" Natasha tilted her head toward Victor. "Do we go in now or should we wait until dark?"

Hardy could tell from her tone she was in favor of raiding the house before dark. Victor's facial expression displayed a different opinion. Hardy felt as if he was caught between two friends, being asked to choose one over the other.

Tactically, it was better to go in under the cover of darkness. If they went now, there was a chance they could be spotted before they made it to the house; however, there was no telling how long the target would be inside. If they waited too long, they could lose their window of opportunity.

Victor raised a huge paw. "All I'm saying is that we need to stay focused. We don't want another incident like..." his voice trailed off, when he realized the implications of his words.

Natasha's eyes narrowed and she glared at Victor. "Go ahead and finish—like the one that got Sergei killed. You think it's *my fault* he's dead, don't you?"

"I didn't say that." Victor was smoothing over his words. "I know he would have—"

Natasha interrupted him. "No, you didn't *say it*, but it was on your mind. You think Sergei might still be alive, if I hadn't been there, distracting him from his job."

"Natasha—"

"Go to hell, Victor." She stormed off toward the trees.

Hardy faced the big man. "What was *that* all about?"

Victor jerked his head toward Natasha, as if to say 'ask her.'

Chapter 14: Guilt

Hardy caught up with Natasha at the tree line. He took hold of her elbow. She spun around, her long hair flying over her shoulder. She glanced at Hardy's hand—still clamped onto her arm—and locked eyes with him.

Hardy's upper body leaned backward. *If looks could kill.* He had been on the receiving end of her fury before and was not looking forward to another round. Still holding her elbow, his other hand shot up. "I just want to talk. What happened back there?"

She yanked her arm away. "It's none of your business." She took a few steps and looked over her shoulder. "You wouldn't understand, anyway."

Hardy skirted around her and blocked her way, but did not make physical contact—he was not entirely convinced she would *not* hit him. "Listen, it may not be any of my business, but I can see that whatever happened is affecting you. And, since we are working together, I should know what is going on—not only for my safety, but for the safety of this team as well."

Natasha started to speak, but stopped.

Hardy saw the muscles in her face relax, while she mulled over his words. He coaxed her. "What happened?"

Natasha crossed her arms in front of her chest. She was not in a mood to talk. Victor had brought back memories she had spent months trying to reconcile. *How dare he?* Cupping her elbow in her left hand, she covered her mouth with her free hand.

Hardy squared his body and clutched her shoulders. "Talk to me, Natasha. What's going on?"

She raised her eyes toward him. She did not intend to tell him anything; however, maybe it would be good to open up to someone, having not spoken with anyone about Sergei's death. She rolled her eyes and let her arms fall to her sides. Natasha relented, "All right, fine," before launching into her story.

Hearing about the explosion that killed Sergei and his teammates, Hardy had flashbacks of the blast that had taken the lives of *his* teammates. The incident was still in the forefront of his mind and had caused him to have the same nightmare almost every night for the past week.

In the nightmare, Hardy saw the faces of his teammates gathered around the table at the tavern. Everyone was laughing, drinking and having a good time. Their faces became distorted and they desperately tried to tell him something. He could not hear anything they were saying. Their mouths were moving, but no sounds could be heard. At that moment, he felt something hit him in the back. The force threw him to the pavement. After that, everything went black.

"That's not all." She turned away from Hardy and folded her arms across her chest. She saw Victor leaning against the SUV and she recalled her harsh words to him. "My father died three weeks before that explosion. Actually, he was killed...killed in an explosion at a bus stop. He wasn't waiting for a bus. He was just walking by..." She closed her eyes and dropped her head to her chest. Seconds later, she whirled around and thrust her finger toward the top of the hill. "And, that son-of-a..." she stopped talking when her voice cracked. First, pausing to get control of her emotions, she finished the sentence, her voice deeper. "He's responsible."

Hardy was at a loss for words. Not only had she lost her boyfriend to Rudin, but her father as well, less than a month apart from each other. He understood why she had been quick-tempered with him and Victor. "Natasha, there was nothing you could have done to save your father, or Sergei."

"I could have at least been there with Sergei. I could have—and should have—gone in with him. I was the reason he was there."

Hardy shook his head, no. "What would that have accomplished? You would have been killed, too."

"At least I would have been there with them. It was my job. I should have been the first one through the door. Instead, they're dead and I'm..." her voice trailed off.

Hearing her last words, Hardy understood the source of her anger—*guilt.* "You're what—still alive? Isn't that what you were going to say?"

Natasha glimpsed Victor, regret filling her heart. If not for him, she might have died in the aftermath of that explosion.

Victor and his team had been en route to the house. By the time he had arrived, the house was in pieces and Natasha was lying on the cold ground, shivering and her body convulsing. Victor had picked her up and taken her to the SUV. Once there, he wrapped her in blankets and kept her warm, while a member of his team drove them to the hospital. The doctors had said if she had spent any more time exposed to the elements, she might have died.

"Natasha, I understand what you're going through." Hardy put his hands on his hips. "You're feeling guilty that you're still alive and those men are dead."

Leveling her eyes on him, her face flush, she snapped, "How do *you* know what I'm going through?"

He held his hand to his chest and shot back at her, his voice on the verge of yelling. "I know, because I lost my team...in an explosion. They all died. Twelve of the best men I've ever known. They're gone," he pointed toward the ground, "and I'm still here." He lowered his voice. "So, yes, I know what you're going through."

Natasha took a half step backward.

"I've felt the guilt you're feeling, now." He held his arms out to his sides. "Every day, I ask myself the same question—what could I have done differently to save them?"

Natasha waited, hoping for insight.

"I still haven't found an answer where I could have changed the outcome of that day." He ran his fingers through his hair and scratched his head.

"Does it get any better?" Her voice was an octave above a whisper. "Does the guilt go away?"

Hardy watched the leaves flutter in the breeze. "I don't think it will ever go away...*completely.*" He paused. "Honestly, I'm not sure I would want it to."

Natasha cocked her head. "What do you mean?"

Hardy dropped his head, his eyes settling on a broken tree branch on the ground. "I carry those men with me every day. Sometimes, I think they carry me when I'm down and need a boost." He kicked the tree branch and looked at her. "My point is you need to find a way to channel your feelings toward something good. Make their lives—your father and Sergei—matter. Let them live on through what you do."

Natasha's eyes bore a hole through Hardy's brain. She saw, no, she felt his pain. He had taken an emotional beating, but he was still on his feet, fighting. He was tough—she thought of the four, dead FSB agents in Moscow—however, he had a softer side, too. She speculated it was a side not many people had seen.

Hardy thought about the funeral service for his men and the priest's words that day. His words had made Hardy think, differently. He debated sharing those words with her. "I don't know if you believe in God or not, but at the funeral service for my teammates, the priest said to the people, 'Never let

70

the fire of the love within them burn out.' For some reason," he shook his head back and forth, slowly, "those words have stuck in my brain and heart. Every day I wake up and every mission I will go on, my men will be with me."

Natasha listened to this American as if she was ten-years-old, sitting at the feet of her father and hanging on his every word. Maybe she was dreaming, but even Hardy's voice, his inflections and pitch almost matched those of her father.

Hardy's eyes met her eyes. "I can't explain it. I do what I do, not only for myself and for my country, but also for them. I know they would have wanted me to go forward and make a difference in this world. If they could have, they *would've* been doing the same thing." Hardy stuffed his hands into the front pockets of his pants.

Several moments of silence passed. A light breeze blew a lock of hair in front of Natasha's face; she brushed it away. "Thanks, Hardy." She touched his shoulder and let her hand slide down his upper arm. "I'm sorry about your team."

He regarded her and nodded. "Thank you."

"Thank you for sharing that with me. I know it must have been hard for you, but I appreciate it." Natasha cranked her head around and spied Victor before turning back to Hardy. She had unfinished business with Victor, but she did not want to abandon Hardy.

He rolled his eyes and head toward Victor. "Go, I'm fine." He saw a faint smile flash across her face before she slipped past him.

Natasha strolled to where Victor was leaning against the SUV, her fingers tucked into the front pockets of her pants. "Look, I'm—"

Victor raised his hand, stopping her. "There's no need to apologize."

"Yes, there is. Friends don't treat each other the way I treated you."

"But, friends forgive each other." Not letting her respond, Victor changed the subject. "Now, let's talk about this raid."

Natasha nodded her head. "Thank you, Victor." She took a couple steps forward and hugged him, his long arms and wide body enveloping her torso.

A few minutes later, Hardy ambled toward them.

Victor gestured toward him. "So, Hardy, now that you've had some time to think it over, when should we raid the house?"

Hardy glanced at Natasha. "My preference is for waiting until dark." Out of the corner of his eye, he saw her body bristle. "However, we may not get a better opportunity than right now."

Victor saw his men coming from the hill. "Maybe, my men can help with this."

Nikolai and Ivan gave a report of the layout of the property as well as any movement in and around the house. Natasha translated for Hardy.

"In that case, I say we go now." Hardy pointed. "We come over the hill from the west and use the setting sun to our advantage. Since it will be at our backs and just above the trees, we should have some cover. Victor, you, Nikolai and Ivan will break off at the bottom of the hill and take a position at the back of the house. Natasha and I will go to the front door. We simultaneously breach both doors, sweep the house and get our man."

Victor contemplated the plan. "All right, I like it." Victor explained the details to Nikolai and Ivan, who nodded their agreement.

All of them began prepping their gear. Victor distributed earpieces to everyone and gave Hardy a small camera attached to a flexible cable. Hardy would use it to scan for bombs or tripwires before breaching the door. After a final check of their gear, they climbed the hill.

Chapter 15: Raid

Squatting on the ridge, Hardy and the others observed the house below. He pointed. "We'll break up at that oak tree and get into position. I'll give two clicks on the radio when we're ready to breach. Five seconds later, we go in hard and fast."

"Got it," said Victor before translating for Nikolai and Ivan.

Natasha adjusted her weapon. "Remember, we need Rudin *alive*."

Hardy looked at her. She nodded. Getting the 'thumbs up' from Victor, Hardy stood. "Go!"

The two teams ran down the hill, single-file and in a low crouch to minimize their visual imprint on the landscape. Hardy was leading, followed by Natasha, Victor, Nikolai and Ivan. At the oak tree, Hardy and Natasha went right, while Victor's team moved to the back door. As Hardy and Natasha rounded the corner of the house, he saw Victor in the process of slipping the flexible camera under the door.

Hardy and Natasha moved alongside the house, staying below the windows. They came around to the front and ascended the stairs, making sure not to step on the broken floorboards of the porch.

Hardy had the flexible camera in his hand by the time he knelt at the door. Sliding the device under the door, he moved it around and watched the screen in front of him. He saw no one inside. There were no signs the door had been rigged to trigger an explosive device. He withdrew the camera wand and stowed it.

Using hand signals, Hardy told Natasha what he had seen and what they were going to do. She nodded, got to her feet and prepared to open the door. She twisted the knob. The door was unlocked.

Hardy gave two clicks over his radio before counting down from five with his hand. When he got to zero, Natasha pushed the door open. Hardy raised his rifle, dashed inside and moved right. Natasha followed and went left. The living room was dark. Mold and mildew filled their nostrils. The beam from their rifles lit up the area in front of them. There was an old coffee table in front of a couch and a reclining chair. They moved around them, sweeping their rifles back and forth. They cleared the living room and moved to the dining room area, where they met Victor's team. Hardy flashed hand signals before he and Natasha went to the right, while Victor's team went the opposite way.

With Hardy in the lead, he and Natasha moved down a narrow hallway, clearing each room. Coming to the last door, he saw it was closed. Hardy was getting ready to kick in the door when he saw the light pattern under the door, break up. Natasha had seen it too. His earpiece crackled.

"All clear," said Victor in Russian and English.

Hardy looked at Natasha, who nodded. He drove his boot into the door and it flew inward. She entered and cleared the left half, while he did the same with the right half.

Chapter 16: Bedroom

The room appeared to be the master bedroom. It was empty. After a quick check under the bed, Natasha moved toward a partially open closet door. With Hardy's rifle pointed at the door, she swung it open and took a step backward. Hardy and Natasha heard a scuffling sound before a scrawny cat came out of the closet, darted between them and out of the bedroom. Natasha relaxed her posture and let her rifle hang from its sling, giving Victor's team the 'all clear.'

Hardy and Natasha met Victor's team in the kitchen. Nikolai and Ivan were opening and closing cabinet doors and rummaging through everything on the floor, while Victor stood at the kitchen table.

"He was here, all right." Victor was scanning the items on the table. "These are components used to make bombs." He held up a cell phone. "He's using a cell phone as the detonator."

Hardy stood on the other side of the table, while Natasha walked to the kitchen counter and stood with her back to Victor.

Hardy was the first to say what everyone must have been thinking. He picked up an empty container of vanilla frosting. "Since when is frosting used to make bombs." There were at least fifty cans scattered around the kitchen. Most were empty, except for a dozen unopened ones.

Victor shrugged his shoulders, continuing to examine the other items.

Hardy stared at the kitchen table. There were items everywhere, including globs of white frosting, except for a rectangular space in front of him. The space was clean.

Natasha leaned against the sink, holding a piece of blue cardstock. "I think I know where Rudin is going." She gave the cardstock to Victor.

Hardy glimpsed them. "What is it?"

Victor skimmed the document. "It's an invitation to a birthday party for the Russian Premier. The party is tonight at nine."

Hardy snapped his fingers. "Of course," he said, his eyes shifting to the table. He stretched out his hands and measured the length and width of the clean spot. "They're going to put the bomb inside a cake. That's why they needed all this frosting." Hardy twisted his upper body. He saw boxes on the floor behind him. "Only thing is...there's no cake. They covered the device with a cardboard box and frosted it."

Natasha observed the boxes and the frosting containers. "Won't it be a dead giveaway when the first person chomps down on a piece of cardboard?"

Hardy shook his head. "The cake was never intended to be *eaten*, so it doesn't have to be real. That means Rudin plans to detonate the bomb before anyone has a chance to cut it, most likely when it's placed in front of the Premier."

Her eyes wide, Natasha pivoted her head back and forth from Hardy to Victor. "We have to warn them."

Hardy held up his hands. "How? You and I are wanted for killing those FSB agents. They won't believe *anything* you have to say. And, I'm a *foreigner.*"

Victor planted his hands on his hips. "This is a big party. The Premier turns fifty this year. Heads-of-state, foreign dignitaries and high-ranking officials will be there."

Natasha joined the men at the table. "All the more reason to warn them."

"Once again," Hardy held out his hands, "How?"

Victor wagged a finger at no one in particular. "I know the man in charge of the Premier's security, General Popovich. I'll call him...tell him I have reason to believe there will be an assassination attempt on the Premier. He'll listen to me." Victor stepped away.

Natasha picked up the invitation. "In the meantime, we need to find a way into this party."

"For fear of sounding like a broken record...how do we do that? You are *definitely* not on *that* guest list."

Flicking the invitation between her fingers, Natasha's mind went back to her adolescent years.

Hardy saw her smiling. "What is it?"

"The party is being held at the Summer Palace."

Hardy bobbed his head. *Okay, sounds like a swanky place.* "So, what?"

"Most everyone is familiar with the Winter Palace in St. Petersburg. It's a large and gorgeous structure, built to portray the might of Imperial Russia. It was the home of the Russian Monarchs, until 1917. In late October of that year, Vladimir Lenin and the Bolsheviks stormed the palace and took control. The soldiers stationed there put up little resistance. After—"

Hardy leaned forward and rested his folded forearms on the table. "What does this history lesson have to do with the birthday party, Natasha?"

"People are *not* familiar with the Summer Palace. It was a favorite retreat for the ruling class during the summer months. As I was saying," she cocked her head at him, "before you interrupted me...After the Bolshevik Revolution in 1917, the Summer Palace was abandoned and neglected."

"For my thirteenth birthday, my father took me there. He said the government had made plans to restore and modernize it. They were going to turn it into a venue for fancy gatherings, royal weddings...*birthday parties for the elite.* It was no longer going to be open to the public." She waved a hand as if she was shooing away a bug. "Anyway, that afternoon, my father and I explored every square inch of that place, including the basement." Natasha smiled, remembering running through the rooms and down the hallways. Having not been cared for in many decades, the palace was in shambles. At the time, she had imagined its former glory, members of royalty, wearing beautiful garments, gliding across the marble floors, dancing and conversing.

Hardy got in her line of sight. "You were saying..."

Her mind came back to the present and she locked eyes with him. "The basement is where we found a secret passageway."

Hardy's eyebrows went up and he stood straight. Whenever the term 'secret passageway' was used, his curiosity was piqued. The allure of finding something hidden intrigued him; however, more importantly, a passageway meant something simpler—a way inside.

Natasha smiled. "I see I have your attention now."

With two fingers, he curled an ear toward her. "I'm all ears."

"My father and I followed that passageway, until we came out on the other side of the hill, far away from the palace. It was common to build secret passageways. In case of attack, the occupants had a way to escape. I think we can use that passageway to get *into* the palace and attend the party."

Victor returned to the table.

His head hanging down, Hardy slowly shook it back and forth, drawing out his words. "I...don't...know, Natasha. It's been a long time, since you were there. How do you know where the entrance is located?"

"The first thing I saw when we came out was a large boulder. There were no other rocks in the area. That one must have been put there to mark the location, in case anyone needed to sneak," she cleared her throat and leaned heavily on the next word, "*inside*."

"What if it's been moved? What if the opening has been sealed shut? The passageway could have collapsed in the last ten years. What if we find the entrance and get to the palace, only to discover the opening on *that* side has been sealed? Those are some big 'what ifs.'"

Natasha noticed Victor. "How'd it go?"

The muscles in Victor's jaw were taut. "Not good," he said, through clenched teeth. "I told him everything we've discovered and that I had good reason to suspect there would be an attempt on the Premier's life and..."

A bad feeling swept over Natasha. "What happened?"

He stared at the table. "Once he found out I was with you," Victor motioned toward Natasha, "he told me you were wanted in the deaths of four FSB agents and I was to bring you in, immediately. If I didn't, then I was going to be charged with insubordination for disobeying a direct order. I would also suffer the same fate that awaits you." He raised his eyebrows. "Whatever that is, I'm not sure."

"Oh, Victor, I'm so sorry I got you involved in this." Natasha put her hand on his shoulder. "I should have never called you."

"No," replied Victor, his voice getting louder. "You are a soldier, defending your country. It is General Popovich who should be sorry." Victor shook his head, disgusted that his friend had become what he is today. "He was a good soldier, too, in his day. I think he has become a part of the political machine, caring more about how he is viewed by his peers, than carrying out his duty."

"Victor, Hardy and I can take it from here." Natasha glanced at Hardy; he nodded his head. "You and your team have done enough. Just give us a head start..."

"You are *not* going anywhere without us." Victor's eyebrows pointed toward the bridge of his nose. "I say 'to hell with Popovich.' I'm a patriot and I will continue to serve my country and my Premier." Victor gestured toward the invitation in Natasha's hand. "What's the plan?"

Hardy informed Victor of Natasha's plan. Victor had reservations, too, voicing the same concerns Hardy had voiced.

She chucked the invitation and Hardy caught it before it slid off the table. "Well, if either of you have a better one, I'd love to hear it." Her head pivoted back and forth from Victor to Hardy. "Anything?"

After more than a minute, Hardy and Victor realized her plan was the best they had and gestured their compliance to each other.

Hardy scanned the invitation. "I don't know how Russians celebrate birthday parties, but in America, a 50th birthday party for our President would be a formal affair." Hardy pinched his shirt between his thumb and forefinger and tugged. "We're not dressed for the occasion."

83

"I think I can take care of that." Once again, Victor had his cell phone out, making a call. He looked Hardy over from head to toe and said, in Russian, "I have a brother who lives nearby. He, too, is a *short* man." Victor, Nikolai and Ivan laughed, while Natasha smiled.

Hardy's eyes went back and forth from Natasha to Victor. "What did he say?"

Natasha pursed her lips and stifled her laughter. "He said his brother, who lives nearby, has a black suit that would fit you."

Hardy knew that was not exactly what Victor had said. Upset, but not with Victor, he was mad at himself for not learning more Russian than a few curse words. It was good; however, that Victor and his men were busting Hardy's chops. That meant they were starting to accept him. And, that was good for morale. He laughed with them.

Chapter 17: Jameson

Once the plan to infiltrate the Summer Palace was finalized, Hardy stepped away and placed a call to Director Jameson; he answered on the first ring.

"Hardy, you're late checking in. How's it going? Have you found Rudin?"

Hardy brought Jameson up to speed on the progress of the mission, including the assassination plot on the Premier's life. The director was not pleased with the last part.

"That wasn't your objective. Let the Russians clean up their own messes. You have a job to do and that job is finding and killing Rudin." Jameson was a man who followed the rulebook to the letter. He and Hardy had made a plan to catch and kill Rudin and get out of the country. Thwarting an assassination attempt was not part of that plan. The way Jameson saw it the additional time spent in country only served to make it easier for something to go wrong.

"I understand the mission, sir. In order to complete it, I need to *find* Rudin, and that involves getting to the Premier. I see our goals and those of our Russian counterparts as being the same. I—"

"Damn it, Hardy," said Jameson, his voice boomed through the phone's speaker. "Is this how it's going to be? I gave you an order. I expect you to carry out that order. I don't expect you to change things as you see fit."

"With all due respect, sir, circumstances in the field change and agents need to pivot when required—"

"Don't lecture me on being a field agent, Hardy. I know events can change. I was in the field, too. Unlike you, however, I didn't change the parameters of the mission. I changed my course-of-action to complete the mission."

Hardy gripped the sat phone tighter. He knew Jameson had a lot of experience, but Hardy was no rookie. He understood the importance of following orders. He also knew that, sometimes, a plan did not work as it had been laid out. A soldier, or field agent, had to make quick decisions based on the changing landscape of the battlefield.

"Are you still there?"

"Yes, sir," replied Hardy.

"Tread carefully, Hardy. Your actions will have a direct impact on your job status. This may end up being your first and *last* mission."

"Yes, sir...I'll contact you again, when I have more information." He disconnected the call. The director had been clear. Hardy may come back to the States no longer in the employ of his country. He pinched the bridge of his nose between his thumb and forefinger and closed his eyes. With his mind on the conversation with Jameson, he did not hear Natasha.

"Is everything okay?"

Not wanting to discuss the call, Hardy nodded and changed the subject. "Are we ready to go?"

Natasha noticed the diversion, but did not push him for details. "First, we have to make a stop at Victor's brother's house. From there, we need to get some supplies before leaving for the Summer Palace. But, yeah, we're good to go."

Chapter 18: Palace

Facing a hill, Natasha stood by the only large boulder in the area. She looked in the direction of the Summer Palace. Tall trees surrounded her and the other members of the team. A few of the setting sun's rays found their way over the hill and through the trees, giving her enough light to identify the landscape. She took fifteen measured steps, stopped and told everyone to fan out and check for the door leading to the secret passageway.

Hardy, Victor, Nikolai, Ivan and Natasha began poking metal rods into the earth, trying to locate the hidden door. After moving up the hill for several meters, they found nothing. They fanned out a little further and repeated the process, going down the hill and ending where they had started.

Hardy stared at Natasha. "Are you sure this is the spot?"

"I'm positive." She pointed at the boulder. "That's the same rock I saw as a teenager." Standing in place, she acted out what had taken place more than a decade earlier. "As soon as I came out of the passageway," she pointed, "I looked straight ahead and saw that rock. It was about fifteen steps away."

"How do you know it was *fifteen* steps?" questioned Hardy.

"I was curious. It's my nature. I started there and paced off the distance," she swung her arm toward the hill, "to the entrance. It took me fifteen steps to get there."

Hardy gave Natasha an onceover, beginning at her feet and ending at her head. "You said it was your thirteenth birthday?"

She nodded her head.

Hardy trotted back to the boulder and stood where she had been standing. He took fifteen half steps and stopped. "Let's start searching from here."

They formed a line and poked their metal rods into the earth, while climbing the hill. They had not taken three steps, when Nikolai's metal rod hit something solid. He poked the rod into the ground in several places. Each time, he was met with resistance, and everyone heard a 'clunking' sound.

They cleared away the dirt and debris, revealing a large iron door. It was four-feet wide, six-feet high and parallel to the slope of the hill. Nikolai and Ivan took hold of the door's latch and tugged. Grunting, they applied more force, while Hardy and Victor each grabbed a corner. The four men were able to loosen the rusted hinges and swing open the door. The earth shook beneath their feet when they let go and the heavy iron slab landed on the ground. Cool, musty air rushed out of the opening to greet them. Natasha tapped the button on the back of her flashlight and directed the beam inside.

The opening was only four-feet high for the first few meters. After that, the passageway rose to more than six-feet in height. The width appeared to be wide enough for two people to walk side-by-side.

"What made you think it was closer to the boulder?" Natasha leaned over and examined the darkness.

Hardy squatted and followed her flashlight's beam. "I figured you're taller now than when you were thirteen-years-old. Your fifteen steps, just now, took you further away from the boulder. In short, we started searching too close to the hill.

Victor held two backpacks.

Hardy stood and strapped on one of the backpacks before adding a tactical helmet and goggles. A small sledgehammer and pickaxe hung near his leg. He turned on the flashlight attached to the helmet and faced Natasha. She was wearing the same gear. They resembled miners more than they did members of a tactical team ready to crash a high-profile birthday party. "Are you ready?" She gave him the 'thumbs-up' sign. "Ordinarily, I'd say 'ladies first,' but in this case..."

Victor put one hand on each of them. "Good luck." When Natasha acknowledged him, he added, "Be careful."

She nodded her head before following Hardy into the blackness.

Chapter 19: Passageway

The passageway had a gradual incline. The air was moist and smelled horrible. It had been musty at the opening, but now it was rank, getting worse the deeper Hardy and Natasha went. Water dripped from the ceiling in places and mold was growing on the walls, ceiling and footpath, which were made of stone.

After twenty minutes, Hardy came to a spot where there was a large expanse of pooled water. He was unsure of the water's depth. He stepped slowly, one footfall at a time, not wanting to drop into a deep hole, possibly a sinkhole that had opened at some point in the last decade. He and Natasha were probably the only ones who had been down here in almost fifteen years.

A few minutes later, they had passed the water and continued forward. There were a few more water pools, but they were smaller and it was obvious they were not concealing a hole.

Hardy stopped when he came to a 'Y' in the passageway. One leg veered off to the left, while the other leg went straight. He shined his handheld flashlight down each leg. "Which way?"

Squinting, Natasha moved her head back and forth, trying to recall the way she and her father had come. At the time, they had been going in the opposite direction. She did not remember the passageway being anything but straight. If she and Hardy chose wrongly, they would lose precious time, having to backtrack.

In the beam of his helmet-mounted flashlight, Hardy saw her indecisiveness. He trusted her instincts. Her memory had gotten them get this far when he had doubted the plan from the beginning. "Natasha?"

"Yeah," she said, studying each route.

"Look at me."

She whipped her head around, her helmet-mounted light shining on his forehead.

"Don't think right now. What's your gut telling you?"

She glanced at the left leg before pointing to the right one. "It's this way."

"All right, let's go."

The corridor seemed to go on forever. They had walked another twenty minutes and still not come to the end.

Natasha was thinking she had made the wrong choice. "Maybe, we should turn around and go back."

Hardy moved forward, never hesitating. He and Natasha had come too far not to see this through.

Less than five minutes later, he stopped when the pathway unceremoniously ended. Hardy shined his flashlight all around the wall in front of him as well as the surrounding area—nothing but stone.

Natasha examined the wall. "Did we miss something or is this a dead end?"

"Well, we've come this far." Hardy removed the pickaxe before setting the backpack on the stone floor. "It would be a shame not to at least knock on the door. Stand back."

He checked the clearances on either side of him. He swung the pickaxe, aiming for the same spot with each swing. Chips of stone flew back at him, striking his face and goggles. He jerked away each time a piece hit him. His pickaxe connected several more times with the wall before he stopped and took a closer look at where he had been aiming. He had made a tiny hole. "Kill your light." He turned off his flashlight. No light was coming from the hole. He put his hand up to the hole and felt a slight breeze. "We broke through. I think there's a chamber on the other side."

Natasha slid her backpack from her shoulders. "I don't believe it." She grabbed her sledgehammer.

"Believe it. You've got good instincts. You need to trust them." He exchanged the pickaxe for the sledgehammer. Taking turns striking the wall, Hardy and Natasha opened a section of the wall big enough for Hardy to squeeze through.

Natasha held up her hand and he stopped. She stuck her head through the opening, the light on her helmet illuminating the cavity. After a quick scan, she snaked her way between the jagged bricks. Hardy tossed in their packs, while she shined her flashlight around the area and confirmed that this was the basement of the Summer Palace. She looked back at the opening she and Hardy had made. At some point, the entrance she and her father had gone through had been covered to keep people from accessing the passageway. She was still staring at it when Hardy contorted his body and made his way inside.

Wiping the sweat from his forehead with his sleeve, he depressed the switch on his flashlight and followed its beam. "Which way do we go from here?"

Natasha got her bearings and pointed. "The staircase should be over there."

Hardy headed in that direction, stopping at the bottom of a stone spiral staircase. With Natasha on his heels, he ascended the stairs, careful not to make too much noise. At the top, a heavy wooden door impeded their progress. Slowly, he twisted the doorknob; it was not locked. He let the doorknob go back to its resting position and motioned for Natasha to go back down the steps.

Once they were standing near the backpacks, she unbuttoned her shirt. "On the other side of that door is a hallway that leads to the kitchen area. We'll need to change here. I doubt if anybody will come down here, but we should stow our gear out of sight."

Hardy nodded, while he took off his goggles and unfastened the strap on his helmet. He stripped out of his tactical clothing and boots, revealing another layer of clothing. He was dressed in a black suit with a white ruffled shirt and a red bowtie. After removing a pair of black dress shoes from his backpack and putting them on, he straightened his suit and bowtie before retrieving a pistol holstered at the small of his back. A quick check of its status later, he tossed the backpack, helmet and goggles through the opening in the wall.

"Hardy, can you give me a hand with this?"

He directed his flashlight toward Natasha's feet. The beam bounced off the floor, casting a glow on her. She was standing with her back to him, holding a fake diamond necklace in her hand. Hardy took it, wrapped it around her slender neck and joined the two ends of the crab-claw clasp.

She spun around. "How do I look?"

Hardy tapped a forefinger to the top of his head. "Is that part of the ensemble?"

Natasha's eyes went upward. "Oops." She was wearing her helmet. Removing the tactical gear, her hair fell. She twisted her head and shoulders several times before running her fingers through the long locks, adding fullness. "Now, how do I look?" Wiggling her fingers, she slid her hand into a black glove that came to rest above her elbow.

Natasha's long, blonde hair, which normally came to the middle of her back, was now black and stopped at her shoulders. Victor's sister-in-law had helped Natasha cut and dye it, in case anyone at the party knew what she looked like. She was wearing a royal blue sleeveless satin dress, the hem coming to her knees. Black nylons and royal blue high-heeled pumps completed her outfit.

Not getting a reply, she glanced at her 'date.' "Do I look that bad?" She tugged on the second glove.

Seeing her dark hair in this light, Hardy had a brief image of Special Agent Cruz flash across his mind. For a split-second, he felt homesick. He had never seen Cruz in any other clothing besides her business attire, slacks and a blazer. He imagined she would look every bit as stunning as Natasha was, now. He blinked his eyes a few times to re-focus his mind on the mission. A thin grin formed on his lips. "You look dressed...*to kill.*"

Natasha returned his smile, while attaching a pair of fake clip-on diamond earrings that dangled more than an inch below her earlobe. "Thanks...You look pretty good, too."

Claiming a small semi-automatic pistol from her backpack and verifying the gun was loaded, she lifted the hem of her dress well above her thigh. A holster, near the innermost part of her left leg, was tucked inside the lace band of her thigh-high stocking. A garter belt helped support the weight of the pistol. She slid the weapon inside the holster and let the dress fall to her knees. Natasha gave Hardy her pack, which he chucked through the opening, while she adjusted her dress and finished primping.

Hardy moved toward the staircase. "Let's go." Natasha followed, her heels clicking on the stone floor.

Chapter 20: Kitchen

Exiting the basement, Natasha led Hardy through the narrow hallway and toward the kitchen. Halfway there, a large man in a brown suit appeared ahead of her. Natasha caught a brief glimpse of a small communication device in his ear. *Security.* Fortunately, he was more concerned with the food on the serving trays than he was with doing his job.

Natasha whirled around, grabbed the lapels on Hardy's suit coat and pushed him against the wall. "Put your arms around me and kiss me." She pressed her lips to his mouth and passionately kissed him.

Hardy tensed. *What is she doing?* Grabbing her shoulders, he pushed.

She dipped her head toward the guard, her eyes burrowing a hole into Hardy's brain, while she barked at him under her breath. "*Kiss* me."

Hardy glanced left and saw the man; he had spotted them. He wrapped his left arm around Natasha's waist and jerked her closer. Their bodies slammed together. He cupped the back of her head and leaned into her.

Hardy and Natasha's lips mashed together. She felt a warm sensation flood her body. Her attention drifted away from the situation. She tasted his lips and felt his strong arms around her. Tugging on the lapels of his suit coat, she kissed him back. Lost in the moment, she nearly forgot about the ruse.

The guard had dropped the food he was holding and was moving toward them. He approached and said, "Chto ty zeds' delayesh'? — *What are you doing here?* Eto zapretnaya zona — *This is a restricted area.*"

The guard's voice brought Natasha's focus back to reality. She spun her head toward the guard, pretending he had startled her. She hunched her shoulders. Covering her mouth, she giggled like a teenage girl.

"Nikto nedopuskayetsya za predely kukhni — *No one is allowed beyond the kitchen*," said the guard.

Natasha took Hardy's hand. When they were even with the guard, she smiled seductively and said, "My sozhaleyem — *We're sorry.* My prosto khoteli nayti mesto gde my mogli by...pobyt'v odinochestve — *We just wanted to find a place where we could...be alone.*"

The guard inspected Hardy, who slapped a goofy grin on his face and shrugged. Still giggling, Natasha dragged Hardy away from the guard.

Once they had moved through the kitchen, they entered the reception area, adjacent to the Great Room of the Summer Palace. Hardy looked over his shoulder to make sure the guard was not following. "That was nice back there."

Natasha licked her lips. The taste of his kiss was still there. She smiled. *Yes, it was.*

"That was some quick thinking. You got us out of a tight spot."

Her smile faded and she felt a dull ache in her chest. "Thanks," she mumbled.

Approaching the archway leading to the Great Room, Hardy held out his arm. "Shall we?"

She glanced at his arm before faking a smile and driving her feelings deeper inside. The mission was all that mattered. She curled her gloved arm under his elbow. Arm in arm with him, she walked into the Great Room, her eyes shifting left and right in search of Rudin.

Chapter 21: Great Room

The Great Room was packed. People were dressed in the finest attire. The men wore black tuxedos with tails and bowties over ruffled shirts. The women displayed everything from conservative evening gowns with low-heeled shoes to risqué mini dresses paired with exotic heels. Really wanting to draw attention, some women had worn high-heeled boots that rose to their thighs. Champagne glasses in hand, people talked along the outside edges of the room, while others slow-danced in the middle.

At the far end of the room, a large stone fireplace captured people's attention the minute they entered the Great Room. The opening was easily ten feet wide and six feet high. A six-inch thick dark wooden mantle stretched across the opening, extending two feet past each side. Large portraits of the ruling class sat on the mantle. The wall around the fireplace was made of stone. The remaining three walls of the room were made of teak paneling and stained a dark color. The floor was white marble, streaks of black crisscrossed throughout it. Four black marble pillars, rising to the ceiling, seemed to serve as unofficial boundary points for those dancing. The ceiling was high above the floor. Large wooden beams, set at specified intervals, crossed the entire width of the room. Beautiful crystal chandeliers were strategically placed to provide a well-balanced amount of light. Dressed in white suits and white gloves, waiters traversed among the guests, offering drinks and hors d'oeuvre's and taking empty champagne glasses. The scene seemed to be taken from the pages of a fairy tale.

Hardy lifted two glasses of champagne from the tray of a passing waiter before giving one to Natasha.

"Thank you." She took a sip.

Hardy scanned the room. "The cake will be easy to spot; Rudin, not so much. We need to move around and get a look at this whole place."

Natasha twisted her left wrist. She had worn a simple, yet elegant, fake diamond watch from the collection of Victor's sister-in-law. "It's almost 8:45— let's split up. We'll meet back here in ten minutes."

"You keep an eye out for Rudin and I'll try to locate the cake."

She nodded her head and slinked off to the right.

Hardy made his way to the left, casually slipping around and in between groups of people. They were talking in many languages in addition to Russian. He smiled and nodded to them in passing. Standing with two others, a young girl in her late teens smiled at him when he approached them. It was clear from her smile she had not brought a date to the event. She grabbed his forearm, and he almost spilled the glass of champagne in his hand.

"Oops." The girl put her hand to her mouth. "I'm so sorry."

Hardy smiled. "No harm done."

"You're American, aren't you?"

"Yes." He looked beyond the girl, searching for the cake.

"It's so good to meet someone else who speaks English." She put her hand on her chest. "I'm Michelle," she pointed to the girls to her right, "and this is Ivanka and Sasha." They smiled at Hardy and gave him a short wave. "They speak very little English."

He flashed another smile, "Aaron," before glancing around again.

"My father works at the embassy here. He's the ambassador. So, naturally he was invited," said Michelle, trying to impress the handsome stranger.

"It was nice meeting you, but I can't stay. I'm looking for someone." Hardy started to walk away, but stopped. "Some birthday party, huh? Where's the cake? You can't have a birthday party without cake. Am I right?"

"Oh, there's cake," said Michelle. "They wheeled it in about half an hour ago." She spun around on the three-inch heels of her boots and pointed toward a small room to the left of the fireplace. "They took it in there. It had vanilla frosting, but I hope it's chocolate cake. Chocolate is my favorite." She grinned at Hardy. "Why don't you stick around and we can share a piece."

Hardy studied Michelle. She was a young girl acting like a grown woman. She was pretty, but immature. He noticed her plump cheeks and saw two small pimples she had covered with makeup. *She's probably not even eighteen yet.* He whipped his head left and right before coming back to her. *She shouldn't be here. If Rudin detonates that bomb...* "You said your father was the ambassador. Is he here tonight?"

"No, he couldn't make it. He gave me his tickets and said I could come."

Good. Hardy squinted at the young girl. "Listen, Michelle, I need to find someone first, but why don't you and your friends head outside." Hardy gestured toward the front doors. "I'll meet you there in a little while." He smiled before adding, "I'll bring cake."

"All right, it's a date." She translated for her friends, while they left and headed toward the front doors.

Hardy walked closer toward the fireplace and glanced at the room where Michelle had said the cake had been taken; he saw it. No one was near it. He thought about checking for explosives, but that would draw too much attention. He made a right turn and continued past the fireplace. The Premier and his top generals were talking. Several of his security guards were nearby, their heads pivoting back and forth, looking for threats. One of them locked eyes with Hardy. If he averted his gaze too quickly, he would draw suspicion. If he stared too long, the guard might assume Hardy was a threat. He maintained eye contact with the guard for two seconds then turned away. Smiling and nodding at people, he headed back to meet Natasha.

Chapter 22: Dancing

Natasha was waiting for Hardy. She saw him coming and met him at the edge of the dance floor. "Any luck?"

He motioned with his head. "The cake's in the room near the fireplace. And, you?"

She shook her head, no. "What do we do?"

Hardy put his hand on the small of her back. "What everyone else is doing...*dance.*" He escorted her to the edge of the crowd. Taking her right hand and putting his right arm around her waist, he led Natasha around the floor, both of them swaying to the gentle music. "We can't make a move on the cake, until we find Rudin. He's got the detonator and he might trigger the bomb if he sees anyone messing with it." In perfect harmony, Hardy and Natasha glided over the marble floor as if they had been dance partners for years. "I think Rudin is waiting for the cake to be brought out to the Premier. We've got until then to locate him." Hardy looked into Natasha's eyes and grinned. "For now, let's try to blend in."

Natasha stared back. He had a firm hold of her. She felt his bulging bicep pressing into her side. The dark stubble on his face would have felt course on her cheek. They moved back and forth, keeping in time to the music. Her eyes fell on the long black gloves around his neck and the silky dress she was wearing. She could not remember the last time she had dressed like this and danced with a man. Hardy was a good dancer. *He's a great dancer.* Light on his feet, he made her feel as if she was floating above the floor. Over his shoulder, she caught a glimpse of one of the waiters and the moment was shattered.

"Slow down." She bobbed her head left and right, searching for the man. He was walking toward the kitchen with a serving tray in his hand. She never took her eyes off him. When the waiter went toward the kitchen, she got a quick look at the side of his face and saw his gold, round eyeglasses. He matched the picture from Rudin's file, perfectly.

Hardy spun her. "What is it?"

"It's Rudin. He's heading for the kitchen." She let go of Hardy and moved past him. A hand latched onto her upper arm, and she was twirled around. "What are you doing? He's getting away."

Hardy was staring at the room near the fireplace. "We've got another problem. They're bringing in the cake."

A man in front of the fireplace clanged a fork against a champagne glass. Everyone stopped dancing and moved closer to the fireplace. The people were standing shoulder to shoulder.

Natasha rotated her head back and forth from the kitchen to the two waiters, pushing the cart with the cake on it. "We can't be in two places at once."

"We'll have to split up." He still had a hold of her arm. He moved around her toward and guided her toward the guests, who were crowding closer to the fireplace. "You get the cake out of here and I'll go after Rudin."

"No, Rudin is mine," she shot back. "I'm taking him down."

"There's no time to argue, Natasha." He gave her a push. "I don't speak Russian, so it's up to you to convince them there's a bomb in that cake and get it the hell out of here. I'll deal with Rudin."

She regarded the partygoers, jammed together, jockeying for a better position. "I'll never make it through that crowd."

"Just start pushing," he trotted backwards, "I'll clear the way," before he spun around and sprinted for the kitchen. Stopping at the entrance to the Great Room and drawing his pistol, he fired several rounds into the ceiling before disappearing from sight.

Everyone on the dance floor scattered, giving Natasha a clear path to the cake.

Hardy ran through the kitchen, his pistol in hand. The waiters and kitchen staff ducked under the counter and jumped onto the counters. Coming to the hallway, where he and Natasha had kissed, he stole a quick look. *There's no way for him to escape that way.* He gained speed and crashed into the only other door in sight. The door flew open and he glanced over his shoulder. Two security guards were following him, shouting at those in their path.

Chapter 23: Van

Hardy spotted Rudin; he was hurrying toward a delivery van, a cell phone in his hand. *He's going to detonate the bomb.* Before the door had closed, Hardy saw the guards were closing the distance. He searched the area and spotted a rectangular trashcan. He dragged the trashcan over to the door and wedged the top part under the doorknob. Lifting his leg, he drove his foot down onto the bottom of the can. Seconds later, the guards slammed into the door, but the trashcan did not move. *That should hold them.*

Hardy focused his attention on Rudin, whose fingers were tapping on the cell phone's screen. Hardy raised his pistol and put the front sight on the cell phone. He took a breath, let out some of the air and held the rest. He slowly pressed the trigger, until the pistol recoiled. He missed the cell phone. The bullet skipped off the delivery van. Sparks shot off the van's side panel.

The report of the gunshot surprised Rudin. The phone slipped out of his hands. Squatting, he drew a weapon of his own and fired at Hardy.

Hardy dove behind a metal dumpster; bullets ricocheted off its side. Instead of peeking out from the same side of the dumpster, Hardy moved to the other side and peered around the edge. He saw

Rudin snatch the phone and climb into the van. From Hardy's angle, he could see all of the van's tires, except for the right-front tire. He steadied his pistol against the solid steel wall to his left and fired three shots, while the van sped away. Each bullet struck a tire, releasing the air it contained with a 'boom.'

The van swerved left and right, accelerating toward the main gate. Rudin had both hands on the wheel, trying to keep the vehicle moving straight. He glanced at the passenger's seat, and the cell phone on it. All Rudin had to do was push the 'send' button to complete his mission; however, self-preservation was at the forefront of his mind. The van veered left and Rudin yanked the steering wheel hard to the right. The two tires on the right side lifted off the ground. The hulking vehicle hung in the air for a few seconds before slamming back down.

Rudin navigated his approach to the main gate. Two security guards were holding up their hands, wanting him to stop. When it became evident the van was not going to stop, they drew their pistols and began firing at the van's windshield. At the last second, they dove out of the vehicle's path, one to the left and one to the right.

Rudin raised his right hand in front of his face as if his hand was going to stop the bullets coming through the windshield. He pushed his foot—and the accelerator—to the floor. The van lunged forward and rammed into the vertical bars of the gate. The speed and weight of the vehicle was too much. The doors swung open, the right one coming off its hinges and landing on the front lawn, several meters away.

Hand over hand, Rudin cranked the steering wheel to the right. The van lurched in the same direction. Its speed and top-heavy weight were too much to overcome. The van heaved to the left, appearing to be suspended. Rudin wrenched the steering wheel back to the left. For a split-second, it seemed as if the van was going to right itself; however, it keeled over, the box banging against the pavement. The vehicle slid forward several lengths, the metal box scraping across the concrete, creating a trail of sparks. Rudin opened his eyes and the first thing he saw was the cell phone.

Chasing the van, Hardy came up from behind the security guards. They saw the pistol in his hands and shouted at him, pointing their pistols at his head. He dropped his weapon and raised his hands into the air. One guard broke away and approached the van, while the other moved toward Hardy. The guard was issuing commands, while taking turns pointing the muzzle of his weapon at Hardy's chest and the driveway. Hardy had taken many men captive during his time in the military and he knew what the guard wanted.

Hardy dropped to his knees, before going prone on the hard surface of the driveway. He waited to feel the cold steel of the handcuffs around his wrists. *I wonder if they use zip ties, too.* A loud explosion came from over his shoulder. His hand shot to protect his head. Cranking his head toward the blast, he saw smoke rising from the palace. Two boots appeared in his line of sight followed by a hand. Hardy tilted his head back. "Victor?"

Chapter 24: Smoke

Victor and his team had been positioned in the woods, outside the main gate. They had seen the whole act play out before their eyes. Victor used his status in the Spetsnaz to convince the security guards that Hardy was with him, while Nikolai and Ivan moved to the van. Before they were able to secure him, Rudin had detonated the bomb.

Hardy grabbed Victor's hand and the big man hoisted him to his feet.

"Are you okay?"

Hardy nodded.

"Where's Natasha?"

Hardy gaped at the palace. The gray smoke had gotten thicker. He bolted toward the front door. Coming to the steps, he took them three at a time. Glimpsing Michelle and her friends, he saw the look of abject terror on their faces. Other than that, they were fine. Racing past them, he shouted and flung his arm at them. "Get out of here." If there was a secondary explosion, he wanted them far away.

Making it to the Great Room, all he saw was smoke. He plucked the handkerchief from his breast pocket and covered his nose and mouth. He pushed forward. People were stumbling, holding each other, while heading for the front door. Their blank faces were dirty, as they used their hands to shield their noses from the smoke. Men had their arms around women's waists, helping them exit the blast zone. Waiters were tending to the injured. Beneath the screams and cries for help, constant coughing could be heard.

With Victor a step behind, Hardy stopped at the fireplace. He took the handkerchief away from his face and shouted Natasha's name several times, coughing in between calls. He got on his knees and looked left and right of the fireplace. There was so much smoke that everything appeared black. His eyes started to burn.

Victor motioned. "I'll look over here."

"Wait," shouted Hardy. "I think I see her. Follow me." Hardy had caught a glimpse of royal blue fabric. He kept low and moved parallel to the fireplace, stepping over and around chunks of stone. Outside a small room, where the smoke was thickest, he saw one of the Premier's security guards lying face down on a woman with black hair. Of course, with so much blackness all around, she could have been a blonde for all Hardy knew. She was on her back. The guard on top had a large gash on the back of his blood-soaked head. Crimson streams ran down the side of his face, dripping onto the woman's dress. Drawing closer, Hardy saw the woman's face. *Natasha.* It appeared as if the guard had shielded her from the blast before being hit by one of the large pieces of stone on the floor around her. He felt for a pulse on the guard. He was dead. "Help me." Hardy pushed, while Victor wrenched on the guard's arm, until Natasha was free of the corpse.

Hardy leaned over and put his ear to her nose and mouth. While staring past her shoes, he listened for a breath.

Victor examined her body. "I don't see any wounds." He took her wrist in his hand. "I've got a pulse."

"She's not breathing." Hardy coughed. "We've got to move her away," he coughed again, "from here." He slipped his hands under her armpits. Staying in a crouch, he lifted her upper body and began walking backwards toward the center of the room. Natasha's head rested against his belly. Victor grabbed her knees and hoisted them.

The men carried Natasha away from the thickest of the smoke and placed her on the floor. Hardy put his hand under her neck and raised it to clear her oxygen pathway. He leaned over, opened her mouth and ran his forefinger all around the inside of her mouth, making sure there were no foreign objects. He pinched her nose with his right thumb and forefinger, took a deep breath and blew into her mouth. Out of the corner of his eye, he saw her chest rise. He turned his head to the side, sucked in more oxygen and blew into her mouth. He fought to suppress a cough. He repeated the procedure several times, stopping periodically to put his ear to her nose and mouth. She wasn't breathing.

Kneeling on the other side of Natasha, Victor held her wrist. "Her pulse is weak."

"Damn it," said Hardy, shoving Victor and swinging his leg over Natasha as if he was mounting a horse. Straddling her, he slipped his fingers inside the neckline of her dress and wrenched on it. The satin dress yielded to the force, splitting open to below her belly button and exposing her bra and underwear. He slid his fingers under her bra, between her breasts. Finding the area where her ribcage came together, above her stomach. He moved his fingers a couple inches higher, while raising his left fist above his head. Using the middle finger as an aiming point, he gathered all of his strength into his left arm and started to drive his fist toward her chest.

Before he could deliver a blow, Victor clamped onto Hardy's fist with both hands.

"What the hell are you doing? Let go of my arm." Hardy was enraged, his voice hoarse from inhaling smoke. Natasha was dying and he had to save her. He cocked his right arm and prepared to knock the giant into next Tuesday, if that was possible.

"Look." Victor gestured toward Natasha.

His arm poised to strike, Hardy eyed Natasha. She was rolling her head back and forth on the floor, coughing and gagging. Her head came away from the floor with every cough. She gasped for air. Her eyes opened and closed several times.

Victor slid across the floor and lifted her head and shoulders, cradling her in his arms. "You gave us quite a scare, you know that?" He pushed the hair out of her eyes and wiped dirt from her face.

She looked at him and managed a slight smile. She tried to speak, but was stopped by another bout of coughing, her body twisting.

After several minutes, Natasha was able to keep her eyes open and her coughing became more infrequent. Her eyes focused on Hardy, who was still straddling her. Breathing heavily, his chest rose and fell. Her eyes moved further down his frame. Below his groin, she spotted her underwear and the remnants of the dress. Her eyes meeting his, she pointed a finger at their adjoining nether regions. "I don't know how things are done in America." She let out a half laugh/half cough. "In this country, however, *one dance* doesn't get you to first base."

His hands fumbling with the torn fabric, Hardy covered her exposed skin as best he could. "Actually, that's not first base. First base is—" He waved his hand, "Never mind." He removed his jacket and handed it to Victor before rolling to his right and collapsing beside her.

Victor moved out from under her and placed her head on Hardy's jacket, which Victor had crumpled into a ball. He put his forefinger under her chin and tilted her head backward. "I'm going to help the others." He shifted his gaze to Hardy and pointed his finger at him. "You," he said, before pointing at Natasha, never taking his eyes off Hardy, "Stay with her."

"Understood," replied Hardy, not offended by the commanding tone in Victor's voice.

When Victor had gone, Natasha rolled her head toward Hardy. "Did you get Rudin?"

"He's in custody." A few moments passed, giving Hardy time to think. He felt guilty for sending her to take care of the bomb. She could have been killed. "Listen, I'm sorry. I should have been the one to go for the bomb."

She rolled her head back and forth. "No, you were right. Even though I speak Russian, I had a hell of a time getting someone to listen to me. If you had been there, they would have shot you on sight." She rolled her head to face him. "By the way, what were you thinking—discharging your weapon like that? I'm surprised the security guards didn't shoot you. That was crazy."

Hardy agreed. "Yes, but it was effective. And, for the record, the security guards *did* try to shoot me."

Natasha plopped her hand onto his forearm. "I'm glad you're all right." Coughing, she pulled her hand away and covered her mouth. "Thank you for your help. I'm not sure I could have gotten Rudin *and* saved the Premier's life."

Hardy re-called their heated conversation along the side of the road. He rotated his head toward her, a devilish grin on his face. "So, maybe Americans aren't so *selfish* and *self-centered* after all."

Without moving her head, Natasha shifted her eyes toward Hardy and saw his grin. The corners of her mouth slowly lifted to form a smile before a burst of laughter followed. She was still laughing when Michelle, the girl from the party, appeared and knelt next to Natasha. Her two friends were with her.

Hardy lifted his torso from the floor and leaned on his elbows. "Michelle, I told you to get away from this place. What the hell are you doing here?" His voice was hoarse, making his words sound even more scolding.

"I couldn't turn my back on these people. If it hadn't been for you," she glanced over her shoulder at her friends and came back to him, "we might have been lying where you are right now." She leaned forward and helped Natasha sit up. "Come on, let's get you out of here." She draped Natasha's right arm around her neck, while slipping her left arm around Natasha's waist. Michelle's friends helped from the other side. Together, the three of them helped her stand. Michelle pointed at Hardy, who was on his feet. "As soon as I saw you, I knew you were some kind of secret agent. My dad taught me how to recognize a spy when I saw one. Don't worry. Your secret's safe with me."

Hardy smiled at the girl. She had no idea what she was saying. Her innocence was both amusing and refreshing. One thing was for sure; she had a good heart, risking her own safety to help others. The world needed more people like her. He saw Natasha grinning at him. "Yeah, I'm a regular *secret agent man.*" Natasha snickered, while everyone shuffled out of the palace.

Chapter 25: Airport

Hardy stood at the base of the staircase leading to a
small jet. The Russian Premier had arranged for the
private aircraft to fly Hardy back to the United
States. It was a small token of gratitude,
acknowledging his part in saving the Premier's life.
The Russian leader had also awarded him the Hero
of the Russian Federation, the highest honor that
could be bestowed on a Russian citizen or foreign
national.

"The Premier wanted me to tell you how grateful
he is for your help." Natasha handed Hardy a box.
"He wanted to present this to you in person, during
a formal ceremony; however, he respects your
request to maintain a low profile."

Hardy opened the box. Inside was a gold star
attached to a red, white and blue ribbon. The artifact
was the official medal given to recipients of the Hero
of the Russian Federation. He nodded his head and
closed the box. "Please give the Premier my
regards."

"He also wanted me to tell you that if you ever needed anything, and he was in a position to be of assistance, you should contact him."

Victor stood next to Natasha. "The same goes for us." He glanced over his shoulder at Nikolai and Ivan. "If you ever need our help, we will be there." Victor, Nikolai and Ivan shook Hardy's hand before each one gave him a kiss on each cheek. "Have a safe flight, my friend." Victor and his team walked away, leaving Hardy alone with Natasha.

She folded her arms over her chest and tipped her head toward the men. "Well, you've managed to endear yourself to some good people. He meant what he said, you know. I've seen it myself. No matter where you are in the world, he will be there for you."

Hardy stared past her shoulder at his new companions. "Judging from their devotion to you, I believe it."

Natasha glanced at the pavement, not looking at anything in particular. A gentle breeze blew strands of hair across her face. She pushed the locks behind her ear. "I found out this morning that Rudin gave officials the identity of the man who had orchestrated the bombings."

Hardy leaned closer, straining to hear her. A nearby jet engine roared when the aircraft accelerated down the runway.

Natasha raised her voice. "It was General Popovich. He was at the birthday party and left moments before the cake was wheeled out and placed in front of the Premier. Also, he was the one who sent those FSB agents to the café. Not sure what his motives were, but every officer in the country will be searching for him. He won't get far." She shifted her weight to her other shoe, a low-heeled, black pump. "As for Rudin," the noise from the plane died and her voice returned to a normal level, "he won't ever see the light of day again. I know you wanted him dead, Hardy, but he'll never make or sell another bomb."

"I suppose that's just as good." Hardy was unsure if his superiors would see it the same way.

More moments of silence passed between them. Jets took off and landed in the background. The wind blew stronger.

"Well, I guess I should be going." He pivoted to the left and put a hand on the staircase railing.

Natasha's stomach twisted. She stretched out a hand toward him, but quickly retracted it. Seeing him turn his back, an empty feeling washed over her. It was time to face the truth. He was leaving and she did not want that. *But, why? I hardly know him.* It had been three months since Sergei's death; however, it seemed like only yesterday that she and he were together. Being with Hardy these past couple of days had brought back the feelings of joy and happiness she had with her boyfriend. Hardy's kiss at the palace rushed into her mind. That kiss had meant something to her, but he did not seem to share the same feelings. Her heart told her to kiss him again—to either confirm or deny there was something between them. Her mind, however, was telling her not to put a strain on a good friendship. In the end, impulses won out over rational thinking.

Natasha curled her fingers around his arm and pulled gently, until he faced her. She placed her right hand over his left pectoral muscle and tilted her head backward. Her eyes going back and forth from his eyes to his lips, she leaned closer, only a few inches separated them. Staring into his eyes, she froze. Something in them said her kiss would not be received well. No, she sensed his mind was on something else. She pulled away and patted his chest twice. "It was good working with you, Hardy. Take care of yourself." She stepped back and dropped her gaze. "And, if you're ever anywhere even remotely close to Moscow," she looked up and forced a smile, "I would be deeply hurt if you didn't contact me." She stuck out her hand. "Have a safe trip."

Hardy was no fool. At the palace, he had felt the passion in Natasha's kiss. She had been reluctant to pull away from him then just as she was now. Though their relationship had started out cold, they had experienced combat together, and combat had a way of forging close bonds in a short time. He thought of her lying on the floor at the palace, not breathing. His heart ached and he would have done anything to save her life.

Hardy took a step forward, past the handshake, and put his hands on her waist; she put hers on his chest, arching her back slightly. "Natasha, I'm going home to a woman I met a week ago and I can't wait to see her and spend as much time as I can with her. My heart beats faster just thinking about it." Natasha lowered her gaze. Gently placing the pad of his forefinger under her chin, he lifted.

Natasha forced herself to make eye contact. She was rewarded with the same beautiful blue eyes that had captivated her when they first met at the café.

"I care a great deal for you. I really do...just not in that way." He paused. "The last thing I want is to hurt you. But, we've been through too much for me not to be honest with you."

Natasha stood still. Her heart thumped in her chest. His words brought pain and comfort. A relationship with him was not going to happen. In time, she would be okay. So much pain had consumed the past few months of her life. Right here, right now...all she wanted was to feel his hands on her waist, and the beating of his heart on her palm for a little longer. After more than a minute, but before the moment became awkward, she cupped the back of his neck, rose to her tiptoes and kissed him on the cheek. "Thank you...for being honest." She lowered her heels to the pavement and pointed a finger at him. "I will *still* be upset," she poked him in the chest, "if I find out you were in Moscow and didn't call me."

Hardy chuckled, gave Natasha a hug and kissed her cheek. "I promise I'll call if I'm ever in the area." He walked up the staircase. At the cabin door, he turned and waved before vanishing into the aircraft.

Ten minutes later, the jet taxied toward the runway, next in line to depart. As the plane made a left turn, Hardy peered out the window. He saw

Natasha standing in the same spot where they had said their 'good-byes.' The jet's engines grew in intensity and the aircraft lunged forward and gained speed. Hardy watched her, until she was too far behind the jet to be seen. He faced forward. He shut his eyes, took a deep breath and let the air slowly leave his lungs. He recalled the events that transpired, since their first encounter. A half grin spread across his face when their heated conversation came to mind. Once they had ironed out their differences, they had made a good team.

Hardy's chest felt tight; he rubbed it, thinking he had pulled a muscle. He stopped and cocked his head. He realized in his excitement to be heading home to see Special Agent Cruz, he had not processed the fact he was not leaving behind a team, but good friends. Reconciling the feelings, a greater sensation forced its way through the pain, a sense their paths would cross again.

He opened his eyes, retrieved his sat phone and began searching the Internet for restaurants in Washington D.C. He spent fifteen minutes reading reviews for different establishments. He smiled when he found the restaurant he wanted, the Bourbon Steak, one of the most luxurious restaurants in D.C. It was located inside the Four Seasons Hotel in Georgetown. It would be a perfect place to take Cruz for dinner.

Chapter 26: Washington

July 12th, 7:55 a.m.; the White House

Dressed in the same clothes he had worn to the first meeting with the President—gray suit, white shirt, red tie—Aaron Hardy turned left at the end of the hallway. A secret service agent was escorting him to the Oval Office for an early morning meeting with the President. This was going to be Hardy's first formal contact with anyone, since his return from Russia.

After Hardy's plane had landed on American soil, Director Jameson had called to inform him of the meeting. The phone call had been short and to the point. Hardy had been unable to ascertain Jameson's mood. The man's personality was cold and his demeanor was rigid. Prior to that call, Hardy and the Director had only one face-to-face meeting, and a tense phone conversation from Russia.

Striding toward the Oval Office, Hardy passed several people—secret service agents, staffers and a few unfamiliar to him. All of them had taken special interest in him. One person cranked his head around, as he passed, continuing to stare. From the time he had stepped onto the grounds of the White House, everyone had acted in the same manner.

Their attitude teetered on the brink of admiration and... *'dead man walking.'*

Two secret service agents, standing on either side of the door to the Oval Office, sized up the newcomer, their eyes never leaving Hardy. Reaching the Oval Office, he heard the door to the Cabinet Room, which was down the hall, open. The President entered the hall with the Joint Chiefs of Staff; he was the first to see Hardy. He acknowledged him and continued his conversation with the Vice-Chairman. Rounding the corner of the hallway, the Joint Chiefs of Staff made eye contact with Hardy, nodded their heads and shook his hand. The last to do so was the Commandant of the Marine Corps, Wesley McIntosh, a four-star general.

General McIntosh was in his mid-sixties and bald, except for a patch of gray hair that surrounded the back of his head near his neck. The numerous medals on his uniform were proof of his professional prowess, having spent almost fifty years serving in the Marine Corps. He had seen action as a foot soldier in Vietnam and as a colonel in the first Gulf War before playing a major role in coordinating the invasion of Iraq in 2003. After the President had nominated him to be a Joint Chief, he was easily confirmed by the Senate. General McIntosh shook Hardy's hand the longest. "As a fellow Marine, I'm damn proud of you, son."

Hardy's eyebrows furled downward, while he shook McIntosh's hand. "Thank you...sir."

After McIntosh had left, Hardy saw the President beckoning him toward the Oval Office. Hardy sidestepped the commander in chief and entered the room. FBI Director Jameson and the President's Chief of Staff, Peter Whittaker, were sitting on the couch. Hardy gestured toward the closing door, more specifically, the scene that had unfolded. "Sir, if you don't mind me asking, what was that all about?"

The President put a hand on Hardy's back and extended his free arm. "Come, sit down and I'll tell you all about it." The President strolled to the other couch, directly across from Jameson and Whittaker. He sighed when his body sank into the soft cushions. "After spending an hour in one of those straight-back chairs, this feels pretty darned good."

Hardy shook hands with Whittaker and Jameson before sitting next to the President. He was still unsure of his future. In fact, the greeting he had received from the Joint Chiefs, especially General McIntosh, had only added to the confusion.

Whittaker started the meeting. He was a short, lean man, in his late forties. His black hair was parted on the left side; a thin mustache lay beneath his long, narrow nose. His eyes were small and close together. When he spoke, he had a very distinct Ivy League accent, having grown up in Massachusetts. His words were carefully chosen. The President had tapped Whittaker to be his Chief of Staff, because of his attention to detail. Nothing made it to the President without Whittaker's knowledge. The President respected and trusted Whittaker and allowed him a great deal of latitude in all things related to the Presidency. "Mr. President, I have scheduled a meeting with the Russian Premier for later this month. Considering how nice the weather has been, I thought the Rose Garden or the South Lawn would be appropriate. Of course, we will have this office made ready if the weather does not cooperate."

"Excellent," said the President, who appeared to be very pleased this morning. He shifted his weight to his right hip and crossed his left leg over his right, so he could face Hardy. "Aaron, you have managed to accomplish what no one has been able to do in a long time. Yesterday, the Russian Premier called me, directly. We spoke for a few minutes and talked about two things." The President held up his right forefinger. "One, he was willing to meet with me, regarding the war on terror; specifically, how our two countries might work together to stop future terrorist attacks." He held up two fingers. "Two, he had *high praise* for you."

Hardy raised his eyebrows. He knew the Premier was grateful, but he did not expect his name to come up during such an important phone call. He glimpsed the men sitting on the other couch. Whittaker was smiling, but Jameson was not.

"Your heroic actions, Aaron, have laid the groundwork for the United States and Russia to become allies in this war on terror. And, that meeting...later this month," the President pointed, "the one that Mr. Whittaker was referring to...the Premier requested that *you* be there."

The events of this morning fell into place like tumblers in a lock. The Joint Chiefs all knew about the upcoming meeting between the President and the Premier, and that Hardy had paved the way. He relaxed, feeling somewhat more confident his job was secure. Since he had gotten the call from Jameson, he had been obsessing over this meeting. Opening his eyes this morning, he was sure he was going to be fired.

The President stood—Whittaker, Jameson and Hardy joined him—and extended his hand. "You've done your country a great service, son. I can't tell you how pleased I am that you're working for me." Hardy clasped the President's hand. "Now, if you and Mr. Jameson will let yourselves out, Mr. Whittaker and I need to hammer out the details of the meeting with the Premier."

"Of course, Mr. President."

Jameson nodded, "Sir," before heading toward the door. Hardy followed.

The two men left the Oval Office and walked down the hallway. Neither one said a word. Hardy had to take longer strides to keep pace with Jameson. He sensed something was not right between him and his boss. The tension between them seemed to have gotten worse. As they approached the lobby, Hardy's intuition became fact.

Jameson planted both feet and stopped. Hardy had taken two additional steps before he could halt his momentum. "Everything may have worked out this time," said Jameson. "But, I guarantee that if you continue to go 'rogue' on these missions, you're going to wind up doing irreparable damage to yourself and to your country."

'Rogue?' I followed orders. I accomplished the mission. Hell, I even managed to get a Presidential 'attaboy.'

"I expect my agents to be disciplined and to follow orders when they are in the field. You got lucky, Hardy. If things had gone south and the Premier had been killed, who do you think would have made a perfect target for the Russians to blame?"

"As I said on the phone, sir, circumstances in the field can change and going to 'plan B' does not mean a soldier has gone 'rogue.'" Hardy held up his hand. "I know you have field experience, but with all due respect, how long has it been since you've been in the field, sir?"

Jameson's face and neck darkened. He glanced toward the lobby. He needed to keep his anger under control.

Thinking he had gone too far, Hardy regretted his words. A beat later, he stood taller. *No, I don't regret anything I said.* If he caved now, then Jameson would never respect him. He barreled ahead. "Terrorists don't play by the same rules we've been confined to for years. In order to do my job, I'm going to need to change the rules, too. And, that may mean changing how I carry out the mission, the orders I've been given."

The color of Jameson's face had made it to crimson.

"I assure you, sir, I have no other motive than to do what's best for my country."

"I don't question your motives, Hardy. Your *tactics* are what concern me." Jameson brushed past Hardy and strode toward the lobby.

Hardy watched the man storm off. He shook his head and spoke under his breath, mimicking Jameson. "My *tactics* led to the capture of my target and the saving of innocent life. My *tactics* got a meeting with the Premier of Russia. My *tactics—*" Hardy stopped himself. He was going down a juvenile path. He was above that behavior. *Maybe, I shouldn't have taken this job.* He ushered the thought out of his mind and meandered toward the lobby. He had a dinner date with Special Agent Cruz and wanted none of this to interfere with that. All he wanted was to go home and get some rest. His problems with Jameson could wait.

Chapter 27: Restaurant

Hardy slid the chair away from the table and waited for Special Agent Cruz to sit before he sat across from her. His plane had landed in Washington D.C. on Sunday around one in the afternoon. Exhausted from his travels, he had slept most of the day and had not seen her until a few minutes ago when she arrived at the restaurant. He was excited, almost giddy, to spend time with her. He had made reservations at a nice restaurant and wanted the evening to be perfect.

"This place is amazing." Cruz looked around the restaurant. She had worn a red short-sleeved dress. The hem stopped less than an inch above her knees. Tan-colored nylons and red high-heeled pumps accented the dress. Her long hair was up, tied loosely behind her head.

Hardy was dressed in a pair of khaki casual pants with a white polo shirt and brown loafers. He stared at her, while she admired the atmosphere. He was taking in the atmosphere, too, a different kind of atmosphere. She looked beautiful. In the time they had spent together, she had never dressed like this. As an FBI agent, she usually wore slacks and a blazer, her hair in a ponytail. Tonight, Hardy was seeing a different side to her and he loved it.

Cruz noticed him staring at her. She smiled and tilted her head slightly. "What is it?"

Hardy smiled back. "Nothing, I'm just happy we were able to make this happen." He lifted the bottle of wine he had made sure was waiting for them when they arrived. "Shall I?"

"Of course," she replied, picking up her glass and holding it for him. After he filled it, she thanked him and took a sip before setting the glass on the table. "So," the word was a sentence of its own. "How was your trip?"

Hardy filled his glass and placed it, and the bottle, on the table. He felt his stomach churn. He did not want to discuss where he had been. His whereabouts were a matter of national security and not up for discussion, not with her, not with anyone. "It was good." He changed the subject. "What about you? Is there anything new and exciting happening at the FBI these days?"

She noticed the diversion. It reminded her of the phone conversation they had had before his trip.

During her career, Cruz had developed a keen sense for when people were not being honest with her. This skill had served her well during her investigations; however, she also thought her expertise had contributed to her past failed relationships. She had speculated the men were intimidated by her and left. In reality, maybe her trust issues had driven them away.

Not wanting history repeating itself with Hardy, Cruz did not press for details. "Now, you know I can't talk about my work." She smiled flirtatiously and crossed her right leg over her left. "As they say, 'if I did that, I'd have to kill you.'"

Hardy laughed and reached for his wine flute. He retracted his hand when the waiter stopped at their table. Hardy let Cruz place her order before he asked for a medium-well steak with roasted potatoes and green beans.

"Very good, sir...I'll get those going for you right away." The waiter left.

Hardy and Cruz conversed for the next twenty minutes, talking, laughing and having a great time. Topics of conversation were anything and everything, except work. Both of them were relieved that the subject had not come up again. Hardy refilled their wine goblets. A few seconds later, the waiter returned and set plates of food in front of them. After asking if they needed anything else, he left.

"This looks delicious." Cruz placed both feet on the floor, unfolded a napkin and put it on her lap. She leaned over and breathed in the aroma. "It *smells* delicious, too." Looking at Hardy, she slid her hand across the table, palm up. "Will you say grace with me?"

Hardy glanced at her hand before wrinkling his nose. It wasn't that he did not think there was a God, but rather he did not know for sure. In his line of work, he dealt with facts, not beliefs.

Cruz smiled, knowing he was uncomfortable when it came to matters of faith and God. She glanced at her hand. "Just hold my hand."

Hardy took her hand. *This, I can do.*

Bowing her head, she prayed. "Bless us, O Lord, and these Thy gifts, which we are about to receive from Thy bounty, through Christ, Our Lord. Amen." She squeezed Hardy's hand and let go.

That wasn't so bad. He unfolded his napkin and placed it on his lap. Reaching for his fork, he felt his sat phone vibrating on his hip. Inwardly, Hardy groaned. Not many people had his new number. That meant there was a good chance the caller was Director Jameson.

Cruz heard the buzzing. After the third time, she gestured toward the source of the sound. "Aren't you going to get that?"

Hardy inspected the phone—*Jameson.* "Yes, I should probably take this. I'm sorry." He excused himself before answering the phone and walking away from the table.

Cruz had ordered spaghetti and meatballs with meat sauce. Twirling her fork in the mound of spaghetti on her plate, she watched Hardy. Her investigative nature crept to the forefront of her mind. Judging from his actions, the conversation was tense. At one point, he said something and looked back at her. She smiled at him. He forced a smile and turned away. Her mental synapses were firing. *Who's he talking to? He's definitely not happy.* She saw him end the call and make his way back to their table.

Cruz wiped her mouth with the napkin. "Is everything all right?"

Hardy was focused on the phone in his hand. "Not really." He paused, searching for the right

134

words, but nothing seemed appropriate. "I'm really sorry. That was work on the phone. Something has come up and I need to leave."

"You must have an important job, getting called in after hours." She was unable to mask the disappointment in her voice.

Hardy heard it, too. He stood behind his chair. His eyes went from the plate of food to the bottle of wine to her red dress. He stared at her. She was gorgeous, the best thing to happen to him in a long time. And, he had to leave her. "Look, I'm really sorry—" he did not know what to say next.

It was Cruz's turn to force a smile. "It's all right." She took extra time to fold her napkin before setting it on the table. "I understand." *No, I don't.* Their relationship had started great, but his abrupt trip had left her with more questions than answers. Now, he was back and they were enjoying a wonderful meal and terrific conversation. One phone call later and he has to leave in the middle of dinner. She tried to make light of the situation, even managing an almost sincere smile. "I guess it's a good thing we drove separately."

"I'll make it up to you." He pushed his chair under the table, "I promise," and walked away.

Cruz watched Hardy leave. *I don't even get a kiss goodbye.* As if he had read her thoughts, she watched him spin around and return to her side before leaning over and kissing her cheek. Standing, he turned to leave and she grabbed his hand. "Be careful." *Why did I say that?* Even though she did not know what his job entailed, her gut told her it was dangerous. Hardy smiled and squeezed her hand, "I will," before leaving the restaurant.

....

Email me at alexjander555@gmail.com to receive notifications of new releases and sneak peeks at upcoming books. *Your personal information will never be shared with anyone.*

Thank You

Thank you for purchasing and reading American Influence. I hope you enjoyed reading it as much as I enjoyed writing it. It was fun researching the different areas of Russia, finding locations for the scenes. The book took on a 'James Bond' type feel to it, jumping from Washington, D.C. to Moscow and St. Petersburg. The scene in the secret passageway and the kitchen was especially fun to write.

If you liked American Influence, please take the time to visit your favorite bookseller and leave a review. *Reviews are extremely important to authors.* Your comments help us understand what our readers are thinking and feeling about our work. Your review also helps others in the purchasing process. More purchases means others are enjoying our work and want us to write more books. Your thoughts are critical to our success and the availability of good fiction.

I hope you're looking forward to the next book in the series, Deadly Assignment. For a sneak peek, keep reading.

Sincerely,

Alex J. Ander

Alex J. Ander

Other books by Alex Ander:

Aaron Hardy Patriotic Thrillers:
The Unsanctioned Patriot (Book #1)
American Influence (Book #2)
Deadly Assignment (Book #3)
Patriot Assassin (Book #4)
The Nemesis Protocol (Book #5)
Necessary Means (Book #6)
Foreign Soil (Book #7)

Special Agent Cruz Crime Dramas:
Vengeance Is Mine (Book #1)
Defense of Innocents (Book #2)
Plea for Justice (Book #3)

Standalone:
The President's Man: Aaron Hardy Omnibus 1-3
The President's Man 2: Aaron Hardy Omnibus 4-6
Special Agent Cruz Crime Series
The First Agents

Deadly Assignment

By
Alex Ander

Continue reading for a preview
of the next book in the Aaron Hardy series...

Chapter 1: Charity

Monday, September 16th, 4:37 p.m.; south of Dallas, Texas

Charity Sinclair sat in the backseat of a four-door black sedan, staring at her reflection in the rear-view mirror. Her shoulder-length dark hair, tinged red, was tousled; individual locks and strands stuck out on either side of her head. Her left eye was covered by a large lock; she pushed it away from her face, letting the hair slide between her fingers.

Charity was five-feet, six inches tall and weighed one hundred and fifteen pounds, but her slim figure gave her the appearance of a taller woman with longer legs. The lines of her bust, waist and hips flowed gracefully down her body, creating the outline of an hourglass. Her eyes were dark and large, set beneath dark eyebrows that followed the curvature of her round eyes. Eyeglasses with red plastic frames rested on her short, slender nose. Despite her attractive features, the one characteristic most people saw first was her smile. Her mouth was wide and paired with a full set of lips that Charity loved to color with red lipstick. A broad smile revealed large white teeth, her lips stopping short of showing her gum line. When she smiled, no one could resist the urge to return the gesture. It was her greatest physical quality. Men were enchanted by it. Women were jealous of it. Children were drawn to it.

Charity's eyes shifted to the man in the driver's seat. His chin rested on his chest and his head was cocked slightly to the right. One hand rested on his leg, palm up. The palm was bright red—the result of his efforts to stop the flow of blood from a bullet wound in his chest. She could not avert her eyes from the man. "What have I gotten myself into?" Several moments passed, but the body in the front seat still held her gaze. A nearby crow cawed and she blinked her eyes a couple of times before shutting them. Removing her eyeglasses, she set them on her lap and rubbed her eyes with the heels of her palms. *I've got to do something.* Sitting in the backseat of the sedan was not going to save her life.

Charity slid the bows of her eyeglasses past her ears, placed a hand on the back of the front seat and twisted her upper body. Peering through the back window, she saw no other cars in sight. She opened the back door on the driver's side and stepped out. Her fingers curled over the top of the doorframe and her right foot still inside the vehicle, she whipped her head left and right; her hair flew over one shoulder, and then the other. The road was deserted. Squinting, she gaped through a stand of trees on the other side of the road, her eyes straining to make out a few far away buildings and another road. With no other signs of civilization in the area, the storefronts were her best chance for help. She could not stay here much longer. If those men came, they would kill her for sure this time. They had found her once. They could find her again.

Charity slammed the door and ran across the road. Her thong shower sandals flopped against the heels of her feet. Roused from a late afternoon nap, she only had time to grab the sandals before she was rushed out of the house and pushed into the vehicle. A pair of light blue shorts and a white tank-top shirt accompanied the footwear.

Snaking between two large trees, she went deeper into the woods and disappeared from sight. Stepping over fallen limbs and zigzagging around low-hanging branches, sharp twigs scratched Charity's arms and legs. She felt the waistband of her shorts stretch to the rear, halting her forward progress. She reached around and grabbed her shorts before they were torn from her body. She stepped backwards and released the branch. Her eyes caught sight of the scratches on her arms. She sighed. "This is going to be fun."

For twenty minutes, Charity methodically made her way through the woods, until she emerged on the other side. Waving her hand in front of her face to clear away bothersome bugs, she got on her tiptoes to get a better view of the building she had seen from the road. The structure appeared to be a restaurant, but the sign was obscured. She lifted her right foot off the ground and slapped the back of her calf. A mosquito had enjoyed its last meal. Clearing the air in front of her once more, she entered the field, the only thing standing between her and the restaurant.

Tall blades of grass tickled her bare legs. Charity thought back to the moment that had started her current journey. She shook her head, wishing she had never opened her laptop computer that day. Being the inquisitive type, however, she was compelled to take a closer look at what had been displayed on her computer screen. If she had known then that her life would forever change, she would have closed the laptop and gone to the hotel pool. Without breaking her stride, she picked a red-colored wildflower and brought the blossom to her nose, breathing the aroma. She half laughed. *No, I wouldn't have. That's not me.*

Minutes later, Charity's sandals slapped the concrete parking lot behind the restaurant. In the open, she felt exposed and quickened her pace, her sandals making a 'flop-flop-flop' sound. She tossed the flower aside and ran to the front door.

Chapter 2: Jameson

"Slow down, Charity, and tell me what happened."
FBI Director Phillip Jameson leaned forward in his
chair. Charity was scared and talking fast, taking
deep breaths of air in mid-sentence. Even though he
had heard enough, he let her continue. Her voice
told him she was getting tired. That would calm her
nerves.

"Where are you, Charity?" He picked up a pen
and slid a pad of paper across his desk. He
scribbled. "Listen to me and do exactly what I tell
you." He paused, waiting for an acknowledgment.
"Stay where you are. Do not leave the restaurant.
Don't even go to the bathroom. Stay where you can
be seen at all times. Do you understand me? Good.
I'm sending an agent to pick you up. You will be out
of there and safe within the hour. Remember to stay
visible, Charity. You're going to be all right." Once
Jameson had confirmed she knew what to do, he set
the phone's handset back in the cradle. Removing
his eyeglasses, he tossed them onto the desk. With
his elbows on the desk, he closed his eyes and
rubbed his forehead with his fingers. His eight-hour
workday had just gotten longer.

Jameson had always worked hard. When he was ten, working as a newspaper carrier, he made a decision to give more to his employer than he received. That work ethic carried over to every job he worked, including his current position. He never expected more than his paycheck at the end of the week. As a result, his superiors had taken special notice and promoted him as soon as the opportunity had arisen. Two years ago, when James Conklin became the President of the United States, he had a short list of names, actually one name, for the position of FBI Director—Phillip Jameson.

During his career with the FBI, Jameson had cultivated a no-nonsense attitude. He was a man who brought to bear rock-steady leadership and decision-making skills and always backed up his agents. The fifty-year-old was physically fit, regularly lifting weights and jogging. He was five-feet, eleven inches tall and weighed one hundred and ninety pounds. He was bald and wore rounded, rectangular eyeglasses with thick black frames.

Jameson sat straight, reached into the pocket of his suit coat and plucked his cell phone. In the upper-right corner of the screen, the time was displayed—6:09. He typed a short text message, pressed the 'send' button and put down the phone. Picking up his desk phone, he dialed the cell number of one of his best agents, Special Agent Raychel DelaCruz.

Chapter 3: Ritz

Aaron Hardy reclined in a lounge chair near the outdoor pool at the Ritz-Carlton. The late afternoon sun felt good on his face and bare chest. Contemplating another dip in the pool, he flinched when his satellite phone vibrated on the glass-top table to the right. After swiping a forefinger across the screen, he typed in his password. A new text message appeared from a contact named 'Boss.' Hardy's eyebrows furled downward after he read the short message from Phillip Jameson—'GO WITH CRUZ.' *Go where?*

Still holding the sat phone, he turned his head to the left and observed the woman lying on her stomach in the chair next to him, her arms resting at her sides. She wore a white two-piece bathing suit, the strings of the bikini-style bottom tied at the hips. Her hair was dark and long, matching the skin tone and length of her legs. She was beautiful.

FBI Special Agent Raychel DelaCruz rolled onto her back and got comfortable. Her dark sunglasses blocked the sun, while it made its descent to her left. She closed her eyes and let the sun darken her body. She was Caucasian, but her mixed heritage made the color of her skin darker. She was glad she and

148

Hardy had been able to get away for a few days. After driving from Washington D.C. to Dallas, they had taken Saturday to rest. After a late breakfast on Sunday, they spent the afternoon at a Dallas Cowboys football game. It was mid-September and the Cowboys were hosting the Detroit Lions. Having grown up in Dalhart, a couple of hours north, she had been a lifelong Cowboy's fan. Unfortunately, since she lived and worked in Washington, D.C., finding time to attend a game had become a challenge.

Today, following some light shopping, she and Hardy had spent most of the afternoon by the pool, alternating between sunbathing and swimming. In an hour, they would be travelling to Dalhart to visit her mother. Right now, however, all she wanted was to relax and spend time with Hardy.

A moment later, she heard a familiar song playing—'Holy Spirit' by Francesca Battistelli. *I thought I silenced that.* Removing her sunglasses, she scooped the phone off the table. Since she was going to be on vacation for the next week, it seemed appropriate to change the ringtone on the device to a song by one of her favorite artists.

She tapped the screen and brought the mobile to her ear. "Special Agent Cruz." Even though her real name was DelaCruz, everyone close to her called her Cruz. She had received the name during her time in the military. Her fellow soldiers had joked with her and said that pronouncing her full name was too difficult. They shortened it to Cruz.

"Cruz, it's Director Jameson. I'm sorry to bother you while you're on vacation, but I need you for a 'pick-up and delivery' mission."

Cruz sat up and scooted further back in the lounge chair.

"One of the FBI's safe houses in Texas was breached. To my knowledge, all of the agents were killed."

....

Go to www.amazon.com/author/alex.ander to continue reading Deadly Assignment.